A MAZE IN WAYS

LAKENDRA FORD

A Maze in Ways

Copyright © 2019 by Lakendra Ford

Lakendra Ford
Amazeinways@gmail.com

Second Edition

ISBN 978-1-7342879-1-2

Cover art and design by Tamlyn Design / Gerald Lilliard
Edited by Stephanie J. Hawkins, PhD

All images are used with Permission

TABLE OF CONTENTS

BEGINNINGS ARE ALWAYS THE SIMPLEST!

The troubles my eyes have seen, only the Father could understand. I thank God for His comfort and peace. Of course, it took me a lot of life to understand His grace, but it was all in due time.

My name is Cindy Maze. I was born on a cold Winter's Eve at Hotel Paradise. Ironically it was anything but paradise when I was delivered to this life. I wish I could say I had a joyful welcome into this world, but that was not the case. What is certain, is that my mother was a drug-addicted prostitute, and her loving companion was her pimp. My mother had a choice to make between addiction and me. And let's just say, having a innocent baby girl was not the high she sought. Despite the circumstances, I made it unto thee. Fortunately, somebody decided I wasn't trash. Which is exactly how my mother presented me: in a bloodied, semen-soiled linen, tucked in a milk crate and placed in front of a doorway with a scribbled note attached with the words, "Take it."

I am that "it." And what this "It" had going for her, was the fact that whoever knocked on that door gave me a chance.

Luckily, there was someone who saw that "it" in the crate and received me without hesitation. A woman I would come to know as "Nana". I guess if there were any light from the dark tunnel, it would be the fact that this woman happened to be my Nana. The mother of the mother that I had not known. Her name was Cathy Maze. A kind and spiritual woman who nursed a way a lot of the symptoms a drug-addicted baby would usually have. She was my living angel, and between her and my doctors, they carried me to wellness.

Beating the odds, I escaped being a junkie's abandoned child, but I was still saddled with a small heart murmur and an acute speech impediment. By six years old, I stuttered my way into school, with just a blue and white plaid dress courtesy of a loving Nana and the Salvation Army.

Remembering my first day of school always brings a smile to my face. I recall Nana holding my hand as we walked into this big building. The lady at the front desk, about Nana's age, spoke directly to her with a smile.

"Cathy, it's been awhile since you've brought a child to the first day of school, hasn't it?"

Nana chuckled as she replied, "A woman's job is never done."

The two of them exchanged greetings as teachers lined the children up to go to class. The sound of all the children talking both excited me and scared me but I maintained my cool, not wanting to alarm my Nana like some of the other crying children did with their parents.

"Cindy, over here." The lady standing beside my Nana put a sticker in the shape of an apple on my blouse which read C.I.N.D.Y. She then told me to wave goodbye, which I did, and the smile on Nana's face could have lit the room.

The woman who was my new teacher walked us onto a line, placed in size order and began to say what sounded like very important words looking toward this hanging red, white and blue material. The little white parts I recognized immediately. They were stars. I had seen a lot of those shapes before.

I mumbled along with my right hand raised, but absolutely had no idea what I was saying. Nana used to tell me, if I really wanted to start school I need to know how to sing my alphabets, but she never taught me to remember any type of pledge. Once it was over, each group of kids, line by line were escorted to different areas. My group was escorted down a short hallway and into a classroom.

The teacher sat me right next to a girl named Stephanie. I would never forget that girl. She pulled everything she had from her book bag. With every item, she said, "and my mommy bought me this….and this…"

Stephanie was very colorful and animated. It took but minutes before she would declare me as her best friend in class. With this, I figured I was off to a great start. I had made a best friend in my first hour of school. Or at least I thought I had. But about an hour and fifteen minutes later, it seemed Stephanie had made what she called a "Bester friend." It happened so fast I couldn't really be jealous, but what did impress me into envy was the big box of Crayola crayons she had.

I had only once before experienced the glory of using a real crayon. The ones I had were waxy and broke after one use. I used to wonder if Nana made them herself with the candles she burned in the house. I refrained from sounding ungrateful. It was the best my Nana could afford, so it was good enough for me.

Stephanie quickly became inquisitive. Or should I say nosy? She asked me a tough question that I found difficult to answer. She asked was the lady who brought me to school my mother.

That was the moment that I discovered lying. Even then I understood that the truth would sound more complicated. Without too much hesitation I said, "Yes." Hopefully, her questions would end before we caught the attention of any of the other children we sat next to. The sound of clapping hands came at perfect timing to avoid the rest of this awkward questioning.

The pretty woman introduced herself to the class. "Hello little Ladies and Gents. Welcome to the first grade, my name is Mrs. Dawson."

"Hello Mrs. Dawson!" the class resounded.

It wasn't long before her eyes met directly with mine with a smile. "We are all going to learn each other's name. Let's start with this young princess. Please come to the front," she instructed.

I hesitated to stand, wondering why she would call me first, but as she coached me out of my seat, I knew I had no choice. I walked toward her to the front of the classroom.

"Please tell the class your name and your favorite color," she said with a smile.

I stood facing only her and muttered "My, my name is Cindy." I heard the classroom snicker behind my back at my stutter.

Mrs. Dawson then knelt to me and said, "A voice so sweet should be proud before anyone."

She turned me toward the class and I repeated, "My name is Cindy and I like red."

Feeling relief after making it through what felt like a pop quiz without looking totally stupid, I took my spaghetti legs back to my desk and sat down.

Mrs. Dawson asked the class, "What do we say to Cindy?"

"Hi Cindy," they all responded.

"Well done," Mrs. Dawson said, as she moved on to the next person. I suppose that was the toughest part of my day, because the whole experience afterwards became exciting!

But, like all good things, this day had to come to an end eventually. With the melodies still playing in my head from all of the singing along, I hummed my way right into the arms of Nana as she waited for me outside of the classroom. To my surprise, when Mrs. Dawson saw Nana, they began to hug.

"Cindy did absolutely excellent today, you ought to be proud," Mrs. Dawson said. "She was the very first student to tell all the others her name and her favorite color."

A smile covered Nana's entire face. "I'm so happy she's in your class. That means a lot to me."

"I am very pleased to have her in my class," Mrs. Dawson responded, and then looked down at me with a beaming smile. "See you tomorrow young lady."

"Tell Mrs. Dawson goodbye," Nana said.

"Bye," I said.

Nana and I walked out of the school and made our way home to finish discussing my day. I could feel that hearing about my day made her very happy, so I spared no details. Cookies, milk and stories would become a daily ritual for us. These times made for the moments I would never exchange for anything in the world!

I got more used to the daily ritual of school and time seemed to fly by. We had a big celebration at Thanksgiving and after school was out for the year we prepared for Christmas. I was always fascinated by the bright lights and Christmas trees. Everyone always seemed to be in their most festive mood. People smiled with their eyes when they said hello and I was always anxious to see what gifts I would receive. Nana had decorated a real pretty Christmas tree, the sight of which got me so excited I could hardly wait to open all my presents under the tree.

The morning of Christmas, just as I jumped out of bed and practically ran toward the living room, I heard a voice outside the door of our apartment saying "Mama let me in."

I then heard the clicks as Nana unlocked the door. It all seemed somewhat strange to me so I stood in the hallway hidden from the front door and the living room.

"Child, where have you been?" Nana asked.

"Merry Christmas." the voice replied.

I heard the muffing of the voice say "I'm here" through what sounded like the muffled thickness of Nana's embrace.

Nana then called to her friends and family, "Guess who's home?"

I heard a murmur of mixed responses as they welcomed this stranger. I eased my shoulder to the wall to peep at the commotion.

As I looked into the living room, I observed everyone gathered sitting around a slender-built, dark-complected-woman. She wore outrageously big hair, a knit sweater, black stretch pants and pumps. Her eyes were as black as coal and her fake lashes flickered towards my direction.

"Is that her?" she asked. Nana then signaled for me to come into the living room. I walked slowly pass the knees of my elders and stood directly in front of Nana with a bewildered expression across my face.

"Come here." The lady reached for my limp arms. Giving slight resistance, I looked to Nana for approval.

"Go on gal," Nana said.

This woman now grabbed the both of my hands. Behind me, I could detect the eyes of great aunts and cousins. I could also hear their mumbles as they all seemed as anxious about my reaction as I was.

"Say hey to Mama," The woman said.

My eyes opened wider than my lids could stretch but my mouth locked tight as I struggled to process that word, "Mama."

"Mama," my mind kept repeating but lips would not utter. What is this lady talking about? I thought, as I looked over and reached for my Nana. I mean, I knew I had heard that term before, but never had I used it. The only word I knew was Nana.

"Child, child. You know how to talk." Nana said in a heavy tone masked by a smile. "Say something to your Mama!"

"Ha, hi," I stuttered, still confused about what they asked of me, and curious to why Nana would participate in my lack of understanding. I just did what I was told. Figured I would have more time later to feel confused.

At the first chance I could find to escape, I excused myself from the likes of this gathering and ran to the quiet and privacy of my room. I sat on my bed hoping that Nana would discover me alone and explain everything. But I kept waiting for nothing.

I guess she had become so caught up in hosting her new company, she didn't have time to search for her little May-May.

With no other children of my age to play with, the night seemed to prolong with my boredom. I took advantage of the heaviness of my eyelids to dream myself into a different place. What seemed weird and new was the fact that the woman who came to visit kept entering my thoughts. Something kind of felt familiar about her, but then again something felt strange.

I slept all the way through the night. When morning came I was surprised to see that the same woman from the night before sitting at our kitchen table eating Nana's grits and eggs like she had never eaten before. Mahalia Jackson played on the record player low enough that you could barely hear the skipping on the record. I watched the woman sit back and relax with an expression of satisfaction.

Nana came into the room and broke the silence. "Well, Denise, what's going on with you?"

"Nothing Mama." Denise replied."Just fixing to get my life in order. Mama, I've done changed. I'm clean and planning to give my daughter a better life."

I flinch. I ain't never been nobody's daughter. I'm just May-May, Nana's little angel.

"I'm happy to hear that, child, but parenting is more than a clean moment or sober hour. Parenting takes so much more," Nana said with a slight tone of encouragement.

"Yes, yes Mama I know" she replied. "I see what you've done here and I'm not trying to destroy that. But Mama, you getting up there in age. Besides, I have been working long and hard to fix up. I even joined that helping hand program on Lenox Road."

"Well, I am happy for that Denise," Nana said, "But take it one day at a time and wait for God's guidance. Rome wasn't built in a day."

MY REAL STORY BEGINS

I wake to the clicking of pots in the kitchen. "Nana," I call, but no response. Finally I get up, walk out of my bedroom and approach the kitchen to see Denise sitting at the table peeling potatoes. She looks at me with a grin.

"Morning Sunshine. Breakfast?"

I shook my head "no" as I looked into the dining room.

"Where's Nana?"

"Mama went to the doctors."

"What for?" I said hastily.

"Nothing serious, just a regular checkup, I suppose," she replied hastily.

I walked over to the refrigerator and saw a note pinned to the side. Definitely in Nana's handwriting. I pointed "Did you read this?"

"Yes," Denise replied.

"What it says?" I asked.

"It's just Mama saying that new cereal is at the bottom cabinet for you and to tell you be a good girl."

I grabbed a seat to watch Denise peeling potatoes, while in my mind I was still adjusting to there being another someone in our home.

After sitting through the morning show on television, I decided to go to my room. As soon as I picked up my doll to comb her hair, then there was a loud knocking at the front door. The knock seemed so hasty and sounded so angry that immediately I panicked. I ran to the hallway to see what was happening.

"Lord!" Denise cried out.

She ran quickly toward me and said "Get dressed. You have to sit at the neighbors!" Her voice was so frantic that I knew it was no time to add resistance.

With just my doll in hand, I grabbed a single slipper before Denise whisked me toward the door.

I was surprised to see two of Nana's friends looking very bizarre in the face. They put their arms around Denise as she walked over into my neighbor's apartment.

"What happened?" Ms. Gene asked. What's wrong?"

"Tell you in a bit," Denise responded. "Tell you in a bit."

I heard the door slam. I could always tell when an adult felt something was really wrong. It's like they all would have this awkward face of confusion and worry that always let me know they couldn't comprehend everything happening but that they were trying to pretend differently. I learned to read this in my Nana at a very young age.

Ms. Gene stood at the entrance of her living room and leaned against the wall with her hand on her cheek.

"What going on?" I asked as the first tear fell from my eyes. "Where'd they go?"

Ms. Gene walked over to the television, turned and said "Watch this, relax yourself and try not worry. I am sure it's something small. Besides, your mother will be back soon."

"Have you eaten?" she asked.

"No, but I'm not hungry," I responded as I sat looking at the television that seemed to blur into just lines that ran up and down repeatedly.

My mind was frozen in panic, something didn't feel right. And as the hand on the clock now showed a half past 12pm, I began to worry even more. It had been hours and still no sign of Nana. Where was she? I couldn't wait to tell her how that irresponsible woman just left me to the neighbors and never returned. Maybe then she would do what I had hoped, and ask Denise to leave. I only needed to know when Nana was returning. Soon after, Mrs. Gene's phone rang.

"Yes, yes, what happened?" She sighed. "My God." There was a brief pause, then a click. I knew for sure then that something went wrong. It's like the moment began in slow motion. Ms. Gene walked into the living room where I sat and said, "Cindy grab your things, I'll walk you back down the hall,"

I can see every step I took in the walk down the hall because even then I think I knew that it was the beginning of a long journey for me. In hindsight, I wish I had never left Ms. Gene's. There would have been so much comfort in not knowing what happened.

Still, I continued on toward my home. Ms. Peg, another of Nana's friends, opened the door for me. As I walked inside, I saw some of the same faces at the house for Christmas. But there was one difference, there was no Nana. No smiles and no music. Nothing but a thickness of gloom in the air and the overlapping sounds of small chatter and corner cries. That's when it hit me, NANA... Something was wrong with Nana.

An arm grabbed me to the side and said, "Cindy, you're old enough to understand what I'm going to tell you. But I need you to be strong for Aunty." Strong. That word stabbing at the deepest part of me. The redness of her eyes worried me even more.

"Strong," I said to myself. "How strong?"

Then the words fell from her lips. "Your Nana has just gone on to Heaven. That's why she isn't right here with us right now."

My heart collapsed as I registered her words in my thoughts. Gone on to Heaven? Heaven being where Angels fly and gone meaning away from me forever? It didn't even seem possible. She would never leave me. She couldn't. She just couldn't.

After Nana's death, I spent a good amount of time being traded from home to home. Stability was no more than a fairytale. Well-meaning friends and family would just take me in a couple of months at a time attempting to evade the system. Surprisingly, they accomplished keeping me out of foster care. Or had they? It wasn't like I could call any of the places that I stayed home.

Of course, there was no word from Denise. Word was she went back to drugs, the real love of her life. I can't even say I missed her. I didn't even know her. I just didn't think when I wished her to leave my home, I was also wishing everything that was home to me away.

Still, as a child I guess you go back and forth between emotions because sometimes I hoped she would just show her face. Anything or anyone to remind me of the Maze home. In her absence I dealt with lukewarm welcomes and uncomfortable cots. Believe it or not, after being shifted around so much to different people and their different ways of living, you learn to just appreciate the small things like clean linen, food and heat. I know I did.

I went through junior high in the early eighties and was very awkward. Always being a stranger to the neighborhood wherever I lived, I became introverted in my ways. I talked very little, rarely making friends, as I tried my best to stay out of trouble.

By the eighth grade I had been moved to Brooklyn, living with my mother's second cousin, his wife and kids. His two daughters, Tanya and Dessa, were in the same age group as me. At first, I thought this would be a good place for me. I had tired of living with single people who really knew nothing about raising a child, let alone a teenager. I figured sharing a house with Tanya and Dessa would be like having sisters, something I never had the chance to have as an only child.

Unfortunately, they turned out to be two of the hottest skirts walking in the adolescent world. Tanya and Dessa had a conceit that made Muhammad Ali seem like a pushover. Both were high yellow in complexion, Dessa even having a grayness to her eyes, making me seem like a runaway off the Amistad. I remember they would take every verbal stab at my features as they possibly could. From Monday till Sunday bragging and boasting on whose boyfriend wanted them and how no one wanted a tar looking monkey like me.

Although Nana raised me to have self-pride, it was so much to stay afloat after she died, most days I believed every negative thing about me I heard. Steve, my third cousin and "guardian" tried his best to make me comfortable knowing all I had been through, but still I had little comfort at times. One thing I liked about spending time with Steve was how he would always remind me of the Maze home. He would tell me about how before I was born Nana and my Granddad took him in straight from Georgia and raised him through his teenage years, similar to what he had chosen to do for me.

He would often sit with me at the table after I got home from school and talk of all the funny church stories he recalled about Nana and her friends. Even sharing with me about how funny my Granddad was back in the days.

It was comforting to be reminded of the Maze home, especially when it had begun to seem so long ago. Still, I understood that Steve had a degree of discomfort with me living there with his wife and kids, even though I think if it was up to him he would have let me stay until I was grown.

I could often hear his wife complain of bills and about how he always had to play the hero when it came down to his family. If I didn't have the respect that I was taught to have for adults, I would have had a few choice words for her. If I could only point out to her that it wasn't me running up the bills, but her over-expensive taste in fashion. Crazy, but there would be times that we would be eating peanut butter and jelly sandwiches and she would come in the house with shopping bags of clothes for just herself. She never complained of Steve playing hero while paying the bills she made filling her closet. But I knew much better than to rock the boat and kept my thoughts to myself. Sometimes her words would echo through the walls and straight out of Tanya's mouth. Tanya was the spitting image of her mother but with a worse attitude. Dessa would also make it her business to remind me of how my living in their house took away from them. I always found it ironic that neither of them worked in a pie factory, but they were so budget conscience. If they had really known the private jokes I had in my mind about how they all behaved, surely I would have been out on the street in a minute. I let their insulting laughter and sarcasm play out only because I was out-ranked and outnumbered, but also secretly holding out hope one day they would be visited by a conscience. But some might say that was too much to imagine.

Still, the smart thing for me to do was to keep my peace and keep my head down like I had always done. Taking as little space and attention as possible but secretly praying "Lord give me strength."

DAMNED IF I DO, DAMNED IF I DON'T!

One afternoon, while walking home with Dessa, Tanya and their friends right behind them, I heard one of the girls ask Tanya to go with her to the recreation center on the avenue.

Dessa, being a follower as usual, started in with "Ooh...Ooh yeah-in...Derek and Flow playing in a game at 4pm. Let's go Tanya."

Tanya hushed Dessa with just a look and then turned to me to say "Where you going monkey?"

"Can't go nowhere." She looked at one of her friends with a frown. "Ms. Goodie Two Shoes might drop dime if we ain't going straight to the crib."

Her friend, wearing earrings so big you could hardly see her face, said, "You know snitches catch stitches. I know you rolling ain't you?"

I looked at all of them glaring at me like a grand jury and said, "You all go, I'm heading home."

"That's what I be saying." Dessa shrieked. Now sweetening her tone towards me she continued, "You never want to hang with us. Why don't you stop being so corny and have a little fun. Nobody gets in the house till 6:30 anyways. We'll be back way before then."

By this time we were at the corner between the house and the avenue. The crew had whittled down to just four of us. Anybody with sense had already walked off towards home and there I was left hanging with New York's youngest hoochies. I began to feel the pressure increase.

"I'm not going to snitch. I'll just wait at the house." I said only to be interrupted by Tanya's nasty mouth.

"No, you're coming so I know you won't be telling."

Not feeling I had a choice, I gripped my book bag with both hands, sucked my teeth and said, "Whatever." Oh boy, I repeated in my head over and over, oh boy.

So there we were: all walking together and it wouldn't have been right unless they were trying to draw as much attention as possible to their crazy selves, laughing and talking as loud as they could.

I said to myself, I'm 13, Dessa is 13. Tanya and her friends are 14. Why the heck do we need to be at a rec center where every teenage thug in Brooklyn hangs out and starts trouble? It was so typical of me at that time to feel like the only one with any sense of logic. Maybe I was being old-spirited, but I knew if somebody saw us all the way over here and told on us, I would be in trouble for nothing but failing to ignore Dessa and Tanya's foolishness.

Well, we got to the corner before the rec. We walked right up to the store where a bunch of guys and a couple of crazy-acting girls were crowded. And yes, who suddenly decided she needed something from the store?...Tanya. Ms. Somebody Older Try To Talk To Me, Please!

They all walked inside of the store. I waited outside leaned against the mailbox next to the curb and tried to be inconspicuous, when I heard "oh...oh, who touched my butt?"

Tanya of course. Tanya was well-developed at 14. She was supposed to be a freshman in high school but enjoyed being "Ms. It" in junior high so much she worked it so she was left back.

"Stop playing! I'm not the one who did that!"

Her friend was yelling, "These suckers better stop being disrespectful" which was amazing as she was the Princess of Disrespectful.

I heard a girl's voice between the crowd say "Nobody wants none of y'all nasty broads," and then here comes Dessa. By now the crowd had opened up almost blocking the entrance.

Dessa spoke, "I know you ain't talking with your dirty self," to the girl and I just knew that was it!

I walked over to get a better glimpse with a little bit of panic in my heart. Why did she have to go and try to be smart, I asked myself. But I must admit, I kind of wanted Dessa and Tanya to get beat on a little as payback for all they had done to me. I squeezed through the elbows and shoulders to see Tanya with her book bag on the ground screaming. "What, what, what?"

I reached down, picked up her bag and pulled her arm as to say "Enough, let's go!"

But, oh boy, did that give her more energy. "Get off me.. get off me Cindy," she yelled.

And for whatever reason, she swung at me. Now, I don't know what point she was making to show off but before I had realized it, I swung back and suddenly this turned into the cat fight the tension had been building up to. Dessa pulled on my ponytail in between taking cheap shots and getting hyped from all of the oooh's and aah's of the crowd. I realized in the middle of all the chaos that this had really gotten stupid. I got the best of Tanya which made it worse because I had embarrassed her.

"Break it up, break it up" the store owner screamed. "I'll call de cops."

Suddenly the crowd scattered, leaving me with the furious sisters and all of their threats. The recreation center was now out of the question for me. As I gathered my belongings and walked towards the house having all the nasty words following behind, I wondered where this all would lead.

The madness continued in the house. They plotted and rehearsed how they would explain to their parents all the bleeding, scratches and bruises. The click of the key at the door meant showtime.

"What the hell?" my uncle's wife said.

Dessa ran towards my cousin with her crocodile tears. "Cindy bugged out on us, Daddy."

"What? What?" he said excitingly. "What happened?"

And then Tanya, the drama queen said, "Cindy went off into one of her retarded drug baby spells and started hitting on me and Dessa for no reason."

Her mother looking accusingly at me with a really pale expression. "How dare you!" she said.

"She lying," I cried. "She and Dessa both lying!"

"No kids of mine lie. Steve this is more than enough. Pack her up."

"You haven't even heard the whole story!" he yelled.

But through her rage she screamed, "Now look at you! You don't even believe your own kids! I'm tired of this shit, so you can leave with her."

With the kids crying and fury in the air, I knew what to expect. I'm the wheel that no one needed nor liked. I just walked to my bedroom, sat on my bunk and gazed around knowing my stay here was coming to an end.

Soon after, Steve walked in the room stood across from me with a defeated expression.

"I know you didn't do what they said but you know how facety they all are. I'm sorry!" His apology sounded so unsettling as he sat down on the chair next to the bed.

"Cindy, I've got problems here as you can tell."

I knew just what he meant. For several months, I would watch him have to defend my being there, forever making excuses for me, although I did nothing wrong. Here I go again, I thought. Here I go.

A CHANGE OF HATE

Although after all that commotion they let me stay. But I was on thin ice. With summer break just months away, I had managed to be as discreet in their home as possible. I ate breakfast before they woke and dinner after they slept. I read books and listened to L.L. Cool J's I Need Love in my cassette player. Love is exactly what I needed. It had been so long since I had felt loved for sure. Nana would make it a point to tell me at least twice a day how much she loved me. I even would hear her tell others how much she loved me. I can't count how many times I told her those words back. Now I would give anything to hear and say those words again.

I used my recollection of that feeling to get me through the weeks that passed. I knew that everyone secretly gathered to decide my fate and that I would have no say in my future. I would walk through the apartment and hear Steve's wife gossip to her girlfriends about how my mother was a junkie and that I suffered from emotional problems. Sometimes I think she spoke as if to get brownie points for taking me into the same home she tried to put me out of every day. Her life was a soap opera and all that seemed to concern her was how everybody viewed her and her family.

She kept up high maintenance style to keep up with competition. Louis Vuitton, Benetton and Gucci draped her closets and her kids much the same. To many people she would be considered "Ghetto fabulous". The only difference was the fact that she and Steve were of the few who actually had jobs in the neighborhood. Guess that made her feel even more superior. All I know was her attitude stunk. And I wished I could to say to her, "I can't stand you, Lady. Go choke on something!" But once again, this was my inside voice I kept only in my head.

Summer had neared, so like every year I waited for my family donations toward my summer wardrobe. I never got anything too fashionable. But leave it to me to make the threads of two years ago work. I promised myself that one day when I was older I would spare no expense on my looks. Hey, if you must be miserable, why not look good while doing it? I thought.

Talks had also already began on who would take me in during the summer. It almost didn't matter where I would wind up in the end. It was not like I thought I would enjoy any of the places I could go. Lucky for me, Steve walked in from work one Friday with a number in hand and told me someone asked about me. Both surprised and excited I asked, "Who wants to talk to me?"

"Ms. Dawson" he said.

My smile began to brighten as I would often wonder what happened to her, because she had put so much effort and attention into me in my younger years.

"Ms. Dawson? I'll call her now!" I responded.

Before the second ring, my stomach had already begun to jump as I hoped she would answer.

"Hellɔ," she answered.

"Ms. Dawson" I said with great enthusiasm. "It's me, Cindy."

"Cindy," she said with a voice that only a smile could carry. "Cindy, how's my girl?"

"Okay" I answered.

"Okay," she replied

"What's okay? I'm just anxious for the last day of school."

"How did you do?" she asked with a voice on concern.

"I passed for sure, I knew I would. It wasn't hard," I said.

"Cindy, I spoke to Steve about you taking a trip to Florida with me and my family over the summer. We are going to Disney World and would love if you would come."

"Disney World, Wow." I responded.

"Yes Disney. My nieces and nephews would be happy to have the company. Would you like to come?"

"Of course. When?" I asked.

"Four weeks until we leave. It will be nearly a two-week trip."

"Yes Ms. Dawson. I would love to."

"I will get everything together. But one thing, you just make sure I see your report card."

"Sure," I replied.

"I'll speak to you soon." Mrs. Dawson said.

"Good bye," I responded back happily.

I hung up the phone with such a glow that Tanya's and Dessa's faces showed the greenness of their jealousy.

"Somebody is taking the charity case to a movie?" Tanya asked sarcastically.

"No. Disney World, for your information."

"Disney World, yeah right," Dessa remarked.

Steve, witnessing the tension sprouting came to my defense. "Yes, she is actually."

His wife asked "With whom and who's paying? Not me," she said.

"Ms. Dawson from our old neighborhood offered today," Steve answered.

"Where did you see her at?" his wife asked smartly. "When did you have the time to be over there?" she asked quickly following her first question. From the look in her eyes I knew there was more behind these questions, and it didn't seem to be at all about Disney World. So I walked out of the room.

"There you go again with that bull," I heard Steve murmur.

I knew what drew her suspicion but it was none at all my business. But I do know that Steve would often drive me to the old way and tell me to hang on the block while he would hang with this pretty lady and her little boy. Sometimes I wondered why he would always need to drop something there but, like I said, it was none of my business.

Tanya and Dessa followed me to the bedroom shortly after, trying their best not to appear obviously envious.

Dessa spoke calmly for the first time to me. "This lady only taking you... what's up with that?"

Tanya abruptly interrupted. "Let her go. You know we're going to have a lot of fun with her gone anyway. We could hang at Coney Island every day and chill."

I wanted to say what was Coney Island compared to Disney World, but I ignored her knowing she would say anything to get me started. In her desperation, she would try anything to instigate. This was one trap I would not fall into. I needed this trip too badly to let them give Steve reason for me not to go. Certainly they would have wanted me to be as miserable through the summer as they would be.

I had learned to play off my being upset because they had begun to become so predictable. I knew how to play their game. I had to never be happy, like a ghetto Cinderella story, with them being the two wicked step-sisters.

It was apparent to me it would always be a war of some sort between us, but I refused to let their lack of enthusiasm ruin my joy of getting away. I let the days slowly pass and kept even more to myself as I put my mind on how much fun I would soon have. Most of all, I looked forward to the time I would spend with Mrs. Dawson. I really missed her.

I remained anxious as ever for the time to pass and my vacation to begin. I used most of this waiting time to drift back into my memories. I remember Nana would always say that when I was old enough, she would take me to Africa. She said she had never gone herself, but she looked forward to us going together someday. Clearly the cost to travel was not a luxury she could afford. But I sure did enjoy the look on her face as she would drift into her imagination. And while Disney World was no Motherland, this soon became my version of a perfect vacation. I knew deep down in my heart that Nana used to share these hopes just to assure me that these same blocks and streets wouldn't be all I'd ever live to see. And I loved her for this inspiring hope.

Africa would have been a wonderful trip to take with Nana. Although sometimes she would speak to me about history in ways totally beyond my understanding, I listened with admiration. Hearing her thoughts about the world were some of the few times I had the chance to see my Nana wide-eyed and it felt good to love what she loved. But of all the things she spoke about, what stuck with me the most was the way she would talk about survival. I used to think it was her way of justifying my mom not being present in my life.

For some reason, she always wanted to keep my mother in a highlighted position in my thoughts. I don't believe she understood how much I couldn't grasp the concept of this relationship she wanted for me. That her daughter was just a picture on her night stand. I knew little and cared less about her. Still, I took heed of all the conversations we had, because even at the youngest of age, one can tell when a strong lesson was being taught. After all the disappointments of my young years. Survival is still the word that describes best.

IT'S ABOUT TIME

The weeks quickly passed and finally I awakened one morning ready to leave on my vacation. Mrs. Dawson called to make sure I was packed and ready to go. The closer the time came, the more Tanya and Dessa's envy became apparent.

Their smart remarks and bragging were at an all time high. If I were just a little bit crazy, I might think that I would be missing out on some cool adventures. But please, really though girls? It was not working. Nothing was going to beat Disney World.

The more I heard their voices, the more I looked forward to getting out of there. What used to bother me so much, now just seemed super juvenile. I knew it made them upset that for the first time they wouldn't have me desperately yearning to be included with them. Instead, they wanted to be added into my plans.

Not to sound nasty, but even if I could have invited them, I wouldn't. Only God knows what I had to put up with having these two constantly taunting me. I chose to let them continue being predictable. I had my mind on better days.

Even still, the hours could not pass fast enough. I lay awake through the night waiting for the first glance of sunlight to gleam through the window shades, until finally I could say, "It's here. Today's the day!"

Could I have ever been so prepared? My clothes were laid sharply pressed at the bottom of my bed. Beneath my scarf I hid the slickest ponytail that a rubber band had ever held together, and I was soon to be free. Could I bask in this moment of glory for long? Of course not, because before you knew it the green-eyed sisters awakened early just to make sure that my day began as crummy as they had hoped.

"Cindy, you ain't gotta wake everybody up because you are up. You're so disrespectful," Tanya scowled.

I didn't dignify her with a response. I just grabbed my toothbrush and left the room as though I heard nothing she said.

As I opened the bedroom door my cousin Steve startled me. "Thought it was you. Ready already?" We both smiled. "Well, finish up," he said, as he laid his hand on top of my head. "Mrs. Dawson just called me and said she's on her way."

Now everything seemed to be so real and I still couldn't totally believe it was happening. I walked into the bathroom, closed the door, and ran the water. I took a glance in the mirror and for the first time in a long time I thought I looked pretty decent. No bags under my eyes, baby hair still shaped my edges. And my skin had this certain glow that I hoped wouldn't wash off.

I finished what I had to do and walked into the hallway. I saw Steve's door half cracked and heard Gloria's voice. I chose to be respectful and knocked.

"Morning Gloria," I said.

She looked over at me and began to attack what I had chosen to wear. "You can't find anything better to put on? Your gonna have people thinking nobody dressed you."

Startled by her greeting, I leaned against the door with my face hung.

"She looks good, I like it!" I was happy to hear from Steve, who now stood behind me.

"I picked it for her."

Although he really hadn't, I felt relieved that once again he had my back.

Gloria's eyes rolled back with a grunt and said "Well if that is how she wants to look, fine. Go on and make some oatmeal or something."

I hurried into the kitchen and turned on the television. Less than five minutes later, I heard the knock on the door and Steve answered with a happy tone.

"Mrs. Dawson, good morning!"

"Good morning Steve. Is my girl ready?" she asked.

I threw my bowl in the sink and zoomed to meet her. "Yes Ms. Dawson, here I am."

She smiled as she grabbed for me and gave me a hug. Before I could release from her embrace, Gloria, followed by Dressa and Tanya, strolled into the living room, eager to be introduced. "Mrs. Dawson, this is Gloria, Steve's wife. Dessa and Tanya are their daughters."

"Hey"s and "h"'s overlapped.

"Would you care for some tea or something?" Gloria asked as if to be hospitable.

"Thank you so much for the offer, Gloria, but we really need to get a move on it. My husband is double parked downstairs. If Cindy could grab her things quickly that would be awesome," Mrs. Dawson responded.

"Girls, help Cindy with her things," Gloria said.

I looked back as to say what? but one thing I knew about these people, is when the curtain was up, they sure did know how to act so I kept my mouth shut, eager to get out as soon as possible.

Surprisingly, the girls' act of support almost seemed genuine. An hour ago, I could not have said the same. But without a hint of grudge they both followed me into the room to assist. Tanya even mentioned how she thought that Mrs. Dawson was so pretty.

I looked at Tanya and Dessa's face and for the first time the devil must have taken a rest because they were just cool.

With my bags now put at the door, Mrs. Dawson stood and asked, "Are you ready?"

I replied only with a smile.

"Well okay,"Steve said. "Y'all have a nice trip, call me when y'all get there."

After the goodbyes we were out the door.

The weather outside was beautiful. It made Mrs. Dawson's van sparkle like a diamond. Mrs. Dawson's car looked both new and expensive, confirming my belief that she really had it going on. Surprisingly, it seemed that Mrs. Dawson had told a little lie. There apparently was no husband waiting in the car. She unlocked the door to the driver's side and opened for me to get in. She looked over to me with a grin as she drove off.

Without words we both understood that a lie provided us with our only way of immediate escape. I don't know how she knew, but she understood the problems I had in that house. I was just happy I didn't have to be the one to tell her.

We rode to her home, listening to upbeat hip songs on the radio. I was kind of amazed how she bounced her shoulders and sang along. Just then I knew how hip Mrs. Dawson was. Sure, she always had a sweet and encouraging manner, but she clearly was not too old school. That made me even more comfortable. I knew this would be more like a family vacation. I immediately felt at ease.

We rode and sang along. We chatted easily, and I didn't feel like she was quizzing me. I knew how strongly Gloria felt about talking about what went on in her household, so even though I trusted Mrs. Dawson, I didn't want the chance to slip up and say anything that might get back to her. Besides there would be no way of avoiding speaking of the hell I go through in that house. And I didn't need that emotion to be with me as I met Minnie Mouse at Disney World.

Eventually we pulled up to the front of Mrs. Dawson's house. And, indeed, she had a beautiful house. The block seemed so foreign compared to our Brooklyn streets. It appeared very nice and groomed from the outside. The welcome mat laid right on the doorstep and I felt just that: welcomed.

From the moment she opened the door and I walked in, there were nothing but smiles and greetings. Everyone seemed as if they had known me for a while, and for once in a long while I felt really good. Mrs. Dawson introduced me to the whole crew going on this trip. Everyone made me feel so comfortable that I couldn't wait to be with all of them. Amongst these faces was Mr. Dawson, a handsome and more matured man than I had expected to be my favorite teacher's husband. He had one of the biggest smiles in the room.

He called to me, "Ms. Cindy come over here, sweetheart." He gave me a hug, looked at me then gave me another one. "Happy you're coming," he said. "Tricia spoke very favorably about you and your Nana. I even hear your Nana once was her babysitter."

This was something I hadn't known, but by the look on Mrs. Dawson face I guess it was entirely true.

"Well yeah, Nana loved Mrs. Dawson," I responded.

We stayed only an hour longer before we all packed into the two comfortably seated van and rode on our way. We must have driven that whole day but with all the joking singing and talking the time just seemed to pass by. Eventually the soothing voices of pleasant conversation sent me comfortably to sleep.

I finally woke looking at none other than a sign saying "Disney World: 1 mile."

Talk about excited. I'd been wanting to go Disney World since I was nine years old, so it seemed I was even more excited than the younger ones in the car, having waited that much longer for this day to come.

We pulled up to the hotel, jumped out, stretching and screaming. Mrs. Dawson asked me and her niece Janet to help check in. I walked into the hotel with Mrs. Dawson and Janet directly to the front desk.

The man behind the counter smiled at me. "Aren't you a pretty young lady?" he said.

I smiled as he then looked to Mrs. Dawson and said in a complimenting tone, "Your girls obviously have your genes."

Mrs. Dawson, knowing he was a flirt, thanked him as we all backed off. Walking through this hotel made me feel like I was suddenly rich. Muffins were placed in lobby section open for anyone's enjoyment. Families walked in and by with vibrant colored swimwear. It felt more like summer than I had ever experienced. It was a fantasy come true.

"Cindy," I heard as we walked up toward our rooms. "Let's take this one."

Mrs. Dawson gave a key to Janet and I and we hurried excitingly into our room.

The door barely opened before all the little people we came with joyfully rushed to jump on beds. The room was huge. Double beds lined the pastel-covered walls and mirrors sparkled next to the most beautiful light fixture. I thought to myself this is definitely high class. Just think, after a week of this, why would I ever want to return to that hellish place I had no choice but to call home?

Between days at the pool, afternoons in the park and nights running around the hotel, I stayed pretty much busy the entire trip. I felt so comfortable with the Dawsons. They even did things like talk at the dinner table and read stories to the younger ones in the evening. I volunteered one of the nights to read to the younger ones. Surprisingly they knew each of the stories word for word, but they never lost interest. They thought I was the greatest.

The day finally came when we had to leave. Mr. and Mrs. Dawson took us gift shopping, telling each of us to pick some keepsakes to take home. Janet and I went for identical charm bracelets, t-shirts and keychains promising we would be like sisters. This felt good to me because as pretty as I thought Janet to be, she looked at me equally. No tar-baby jokes, no nappy-head insults, just pure kindness. We even wore our hair the same way, accentuated by our strawberry lip gloss and Minnie Mouse visors.

The last night fell on me hard. As playful and joyous as everyone was, I could not help but to be in a somber mood. I realized this would all soon come to an end. No more smiles and grins. I would be heading back to insults and embarrassment.

Mrs. Dawson picked up on this so before dinner and she asked if I would join her for a walk. We walked until we came to a poolside. She told me to have a seat as she asked me if I had enjoyed myself. I could tell that, despite anything I could have thought of to dismiss this question, she had already known the truth. I guess I could have tried to hide my emotions, but I suppose a part of me wanted her to ask this question. Wanted her to know the answer. "Cindy you've been dragging around like your favorite pet died today. Is there something you would like to talk about?"

"It's nothing, I'm okay," I said.

She then said, "I know better than that. I used to look just like you when I was bothered. Cindy it seems like maybe you're not too excited about going back to Steve's."

"Steve's not the problem but…" I struggled with how not to lie but also not tell the whole truth.

Mrs. Dawson interrupted me and said "I know Cindy. Steve explained everything. I spoke to him earlier when I didn't know what was going on with you and he said it would be best for you at least for the meanwhile to stick with us for the summer. That is, if that's okay with you?"

It was like a fireball of happiness exploded in my chest. "Of course, I would love to!"

I leaned to her with open arms as she held me in a tight grip. She spoke in a low voice and said, "Everything will be fine young lady, just fine."

I could hardly wait to tell Janet the news but by the time we got back to our rooms she was buried in her pillow, sleeping like a baby. I decided to do the same.

Early the next morning we all packed into the van, which meant the end of Disney World, but the continuation of what I thought would be a wonderful new plan for the summer. I imagined the looks Tanya and Dessa would give me when I walked in the house. During the ride back, my imagination ran wild. By the time we arrived at the Dawsons home, Mr. and Ms. Dawson suggested we go back to Steve's to get some more of my regular things from the house. I agreed and we took the detour towards my home. As we turned onto my block, I stared at police cars lined up in front of Steve's house, and the police stood on the stairs and in the doorway. My emotions went into panic.

Surprisingly, the police gave us no hassle. Just a few questions before they let us enter. I walked in to see Steve, his wife and Dessa sitting sorrowfully at the table talking to a stocky black suited detective. The Dawsons stood observantly to the side as they evaluated the commotion.

"What's wrong?" I asked.

With tearful eyes Dessa answered "Tanya's missing."

I could see the death in her eyes. Seeing her look defeated for the first time, I felt nothing but sorrow for their pain.

I overheard Steve explaining to the detective that he had received a frantic call from Tanya around three in the morning. He said that she sobbed uncontrollably, saying, "I don't think they're gonna let me come home. They're hurting me." There had been a loud scream from a male voice and the phone just clicked.

Steve held back tears as his voice muffled with sadness. Dessa and Gloria just held each other with dead tears kept by red eyes. I could tell that they were screaming in silence. My mind rumbled as I imagined Tanya by herself away from home and in strange company. I couldn't imagine her being tough enough to remain calm. This was awful.

Gloria got up and gave me a hug, something she had never done before and gave me a sad smile. I felt her exhaustion as I imagined her waiting sleeplessly since she got the call.

She said, "I hear you're gonna spend some weeks with the Dawsons, do you want to go?"

Suddenly my excitement subsided and I felt remorseful about leaving.

Gloria continued, "Oh of course you do." She smirked. "When you get back, Tanya, Dessa, you and I can get some makeovers for your step up into 9th grade."

I smiled and said, "Yeah, me, you, Tanya and Dessa." I don't know why but I felt inside Tanya wouldn't be with us. But I acted as if I knew she would.

By the time we finished talking, the officers began clearing out the apartment and leaving from the front of the house. Mr. and Mrs. Dawson then waited in the car with my things that had already been packed. I jumped in the car hung my head low too dazed by the events unfolding with Tanya to concentrate. My mind wandered to all the possible things Tanya could be going through right now. Each thought was more frightening than the other.

"Cindy…. Cindy, are you okay?" She asked.

Our eyes met as they began to swell up with tears.

"I'm fine," I answered.

I guess I wasn't convincing enough because her hand extended back towards my face as she spoke the words that could have come straight from my Nana's mouth.

"God has His will so we must trust His way. Your cousin will be home soon enough."

I faked a smile but the concern still lay in my heart. I had experienced God's will before, and His way as He took my Nana away from me. I thought God's way was to make things better not worse. This confused me and gave me little hope for Tanya's return. But conscious of my new living situation, I did not want to burden the Dawsons with any more of my emotional setbacks. I needed to be viewed as young, happy and hopeful, not as a charity case. I wanted to be worthy of their kindness.

We pulled up into a garage I hadn't noticed before. I guess it was a part of their house I'd never paid attention to but it included a door leading to the kitchen.

Mrs. Dawson looked at me with a smile. "So Cindy, this looks like it'll be your home for a while and I want you to make yourself entirely comfortable. You don't have to ask to use, eat or do anything within this house. All we ask is clean after yourself. At 11 o'clock we ask that the TV is off and on Sundays you be ready for church. Is that cool with you?"

"That's all?" I asked.

She nodded in agreement.

Suddenly my mood lightened up as I looked around and felt that sense of welcoming I'd had on my last trip to their house. The Dawsons had expensive taste, something you could tell just by looking at the china in the china closet. Their home was their haven, and although they were only a couple of blocks away from one of the worst projects in Brooklyn, it seemed they lived a world away. This was definitely a nice place to be.

After a cold glass of juice, I walked up the stairs to my new perfectly designed headquarters. This was a place a girl could feel like a girl. I gathered this was where their nieces slept since the Dawsons had no children of their own. I did wonder why they had no children, since they would be perfect parents. And judging by the bunch on our Florida trip, Christmas alone could become very expensive.

I sat on the canopy bed looking around. Clothing space, check. Stereo set, check. Color TV, check. This was truly an upgrade. If I hadn't known better it would seem this room and the Dawsons knew I was coming. Though I knew this wasn't true, a whole summer in this house was a match made in heaven.

"Cindy, everyone is in the family room watching movies and waiting for you to join them, if you'd like," Mrs. Dawson said peeping her head through the door.

"I'll be down in a few," I responded.

"Take your time," she replied.

I stood at the window staring at the perfectly-groomed backyard. It seemed either Mr. or Mrs. Dawson had a passion for gardening. I could tell from the way everything was beautifully coordinated by shape and color that the garden was tended with love. It just gave the home the extra pleasant appeal that added even more comfort.

After watching a movie, everyone began to say their goodbyes, a few at a time. Janet left as well but she promised to return by weekend. After their last family member left, it was just me, the Dawsons and a hamster named Jefferson. I stayed clear of the hamster cage though. He looked too much like a rat to me and as long as he kept his space I would never bother him, gladly staying in mine.

Dinner was pizza, which we all ate watching movies, so after my first shower in the new home I was off to lie on the crisp sheets of the canopy bed. With a little night air from the window and I slept like a baby. Good Night.

UNINVITED GUEST

August came before I was ready. Though July had good days filled with picnics, amusement parks, and my first ever camp out, I hoped it would never end. With school right around the corner, I worried what the new living arrangements would be at Steve's house. Last I heard, the search was still on for Tanya. The hope, however, faded with time. I prayed for her and even sometimes in my dreams I would run into her at the store talking with her friends. I'd even make it my business to invite Dessa out with my friends a few times. She never wanted to come. I heard the depression in her voice and I just wanted to comfort her.

School shopping had already been put into play. I'd received socks, tights, notebooks, and folders from different family members even got a nice set of earrings with the letter C on them. But truthfully, I was ready for the new freshman style. What was in at 12 and 13 was definitely out this year. I hoped someone realized that I looked a little out of date, and offered to put me more in style with my peers.

Just as I began to give myself a makeover in my mind, the doorbell rang. No one seemed to answer, so I went to the door.

"Who is it?" I asked.

"Denise," The person answered.

Still unsure of what I heard, I asked again, "Who is it?"

"Denise," the person said louder.

As I now peeped through the blinds I realize that it was exactly the Denise I hadn't wanted it to be. I thought that this couldn't be How did she find me? I hesitated to open the door, hoping she would just leave.

Right as I hesitated, Mrs. Dawson walked up behind me and said, "Cindy, if you don't answer the door the people might leave."

I stepped aside as she opened the door. "Denise! What a surprise." she said.

"Hey Trish, how are you doing?" Denise responded.

As the door now opened wider to welcome her, Denise walked in with the same fake smile I remembered. That mother of mine in her polyester get up with her head wrapped up like she just came from Africa. She was so out of order.

"Cindy, how's my girl?" she asked in a baby tone.

In my mind I asked her if she was delusional. Talking to me like I was some baby. I was sorely tempted to tell her that she missed out seeing me as a baby, so she needed to stop it. Instead, I just opted not to dignify her with an answer.

Mrs. Dawson spoke in my stead, "She's really good!"

I could tell by the sarcastic twist in Mrs. Dawson tone she too knew this was a headache waiting to happen.

Denise looked up and around. "I see, I see. Trish got her a good one ha… ha," she laughed by herself.

"What brings you by Denise?" Mrs Dawson asked with a light, but stern, tone.

"I got your address from Steve's wife and it's sad what happen to their little girl. They are planning things now."

"What? Tanya?" I asked.

"Y'all have not heard? They found Tanya last night a half mile away from their house in an abandoned brownstone naked and bruised up. Police said who ever had her kept her there not feeding her, raping her repeatedly and lord knows what else."

"So she's still alive ain't she?" Mrs. Dawson said frantically.

"Oh no those sick bastards abused her even after the life was out of her body. It should be all over the news. Everybody's sick behind this."

I walked off towards the bottom step and collapsed to the rail.

"Cindy," Denise walked over. "Baby don't cry," she said.

I felt my breath become short as I wailed silently.

"Get her some water, Trish."

"Oh Jesus," Mrs. Dawson said as she walked towards the kitchen.

Through this shock I still had an uneasy feeling as this deliverer of bad news rubbed and patted my back. I stood and ran up the stairs to the bathroom and threw up every bit of food and fluid I had in me. I couldn't believe this. Tanya, why Tanya?

Denise must have sensed my uncomfortableness with her, so she sent Mrs. Dawson after me. I sat on the floor and leaned towards the toilet as Mrs. Dawson came in the bathroom, closed the door and sat on the floor next to me. She pulled me towards her and began to rock me back and forward.

"It's OK, let it out," she said.

I did just that. Hot tears, runny nose, swelling eyes. I would have never guessed that Tanya's death would hurt me this bad, but it truly had. She wasn't always the kindest to me but now with all that had happened to her, none of that seemed to matter. So young, now so gone. I really saw no reason behind such a heinous event.

I got myself collected enough to wash my face and rinse my mouth with the help of Mrs. Dawson. She walked me into my room, guiding me gently. I could still hear Denise's voice downstairs talking to Mr. Dawson, but I just laid across the bed trying to phase her out. What else did she want? Why was she here? She came around before Nana died now she's back when Tanya dies. She must be the grim reaper, I thought. I wished she would just leave. I just couldn't believe that after more than five years she could just show up out of nowhere and I was supposed to be happy or something. Please, I thought no way. There was a knock on the bedroom door and Mr. Dawson entered.

"Ms. Cindy, how are you doing, princess?"

I lifted my head off my hand and said, "Alright now, thank you."

"So I met your mom. Did you guys catch up a little?"

"No," I said grudgingly.

"Whoa, that didn't sound too happy."

I asked much softer, "Is she still here?"

"No Cindy. We suggested it might be best to stop by tomorrow when you felt better," he said with concern in his voice. "But Cindy," he continued. "From what I am hearing, your mother says Steve and his family have been so devastated by this blow, that she may be taking you with her once school begins."

"What?!" I yelled loudly. "She's a junky! Where would she even take me?" I asked as my fear and rage began to get the better part of me.

"Well I don't know, Sweetie. She claims to have a fiancé with a nice stable place for you. Perhaps it will be nice."

"Perhaps not. Mr. Dawson she's crazy. I don't know her. She just doesn't want me to be happy. That's why she's around." I said with anger boiling under my skin.

"Cindy..."

"No disrespect Mr. Dawson but you don't know her. She is nothing but trouble."

I could see the sympathy in his eyes as he was lost for words. But I was so angry. Denise or Mom or whomever she claimed to be was the last person I wanted to live with. I had to figure something out to stop this from happening. Something quick.

The day of Tanya's funeral, I couldn't eat a thing. After the last funeral, I had nightmares for months. I wasn't ready at all for another one but this was what had to be. Besides it would be the last I would see of Tanya.

We rode in the car that seemed even hotter than the 90 degrees it was outside the car. We listened to the spirituals on the radio as we wept. I didn't ride with the family and, in truth, that was perfectly fine. I felt more comfortable with the Dawsons, and while we approached the church, I wanted more than anything to just mingle amongst these strangers and then retreat to my comfort zone away from all who knew me. I did realize this was wishful thinking though.

I arrived right just in time to join the line of my family behind Tanya's casket. It was a horrible sight. The casket was smaller than average. Cherry oak with a white arrangement on top and a red ribbon that read "Sweet dreams". We marched in as the preacher read scripture and sat in the front while everyone else stood up. I remember looking two rows up and seeing Steve embrace Dessa as she cried. I cried along at that sight.

Poor Dessa. As mean as she'd been to me, I couldn't imagine how she felt. Her only sister, and her closest friend, gone forever. I just wanted to get up and hug her myself. But instead I sat staring at the casket. Tanya looked so pretty lying there. Her hair laid curled against a pretty silk pillow. I imagined her sitting up in the casket and saying, "I'm not dead, what's wrong with y'all?" but she laid there still and silent resting in peace.

During the service, a lot of things were said about Tanya by friends who knew her. About how she wanted to be a nurse or fashion designer. But the preacher took most of the time addressing the state of our communities and how we were losing our young every day. I agreed with many of the things he said, and adults nodded their heads in agreement, as well. But what could we do I asked myself. And was it too late?

After the funeral, we met back at Steve's house. I met a lot of family from Georgia. Steve's father was there with a lot of family.

We ate, talked and cried until the evening came to an end. During this time, I walked into what used to be my bedroom. I sat on the bed looking at where Tanya slept which seemed virtually untouched. My tears had been finished and the reality of her death began to settle over me. All that was left were her teddy bears, diary and the pictures stuck into the side of the mirror. This room was in many ways not the same. I could not hear her voice in it. For the first time, I began to miss it.

After a while, I went back to the Dawsons. Not much was said before I went to my room and went to bed. It had been a long day and rest was well needed. It seemed I slept through the following weeks as well.

Eventually it was almost time for school to start and the question of whether I was moving in with Denise remained unanswered. I saw in Mrs. Dawson's face that she really didn't want me to go either. For the past two months, we'd all been like a happy little family. I prayed it would never end. I mean, God knew this was the best place for me, didn't He? This was the first place I'd felt comfortable since leaving the Maze home. I didn't want to give it up, not even if it was to go with my so-called mother.

Every day that passed meant uncertainty for me. It started to feel like this home was just a teaser. A sick joke to remind me of the peace I could never keep. You would think I would be used to this by now but in truth, there is no getting used to being shipped around. I sometimes wondered if a group home would have seemed more stable.

I let the week roll by slowly as Mrs. Dawson and I both looked forward to school, me learning and her teaching. The only thing that gave me some kind of comfort was knowing I would be changing schools. Since my transfer would be to another district, my step up to 9th grade would be to a real high school. I heard high school was another world.

Anyway, two nights before the school year began Denise came back around. She arrived early one afternoon talking about she wanted me to come with her. I was hesitant and so were the Dawsons, but we all knew I would have to get used to being around this woman.

I got dressed and left the house with my mother. Outside there was a nice gray car that we walked towards. I knew it couldn't be hers, besides there was somebody else in the car already. But she jumped in the passenger seat as I opened the back door. Easing into the car I noticed that sitting in the seat next to me was this cute brown skinny little boy, all buckled up. He looked to be about two or three years old and he had a little wrestling man in his hands. He was adorable. Before I could ask about him, Denise introduced me to the man driving this Cadillac.

"Cindy, this is Richie, my fiance. And this little guy back there with you is also named Richie. That's our little boy and your brother."

I looked at them with half a smile, wondering all the while when she got clean enough to have a baby and how she could all of a sudden get clean enough to raise a child when she just dropped me in a milk crate almost fourteen years ago. I didn't say out loud what I thought but I believe she caught my vibe. And this guy, Big Richie, what was he doing with her? I thought he must not know her real history. Big Richie was light-skinned, and even though he was driving I could tell he was a very tall, muscular man who had a very serious look on his face. He spoke to me, but I could tell he wasn't the talkative type. And I surely didn't put on the impression that I was either.

As we rode, anxiety, anger and curiosity all boiled inside of me. I was forced to tolerate Denise's exaggerations about how wonderful Big Richie was. All the while I was asking myself what could she possibly know about me? Why was she trying to sell me to this guy?

In almost a blur I realized that they were taking me to a department store and I tried my best to keep up with this charade.

"Cindy this would look so nice on you, try this on. Oh, oh that so cute honey," she said.

I wondered if I should feel happy to play dress up with this lady? Obviously, she was in a full-fledged acting role, but what part did I play? And oh, Mr. Showboat Big Richie, pulling out wads of money as my mom draped his arm like he was a king or something, what was he playing at? Then, I got it. The four of us were pretending to be a happy well-adjusted family. Applause for the great show, but I didn't know these people. Yeah, I gladly accepted the clothes; but I did not believe for one bit that this was the beginning of a happy story.

LET'S PLAY PRETEND, RIGHT?

Though my subconscious tried to convince me to just accept my mother's new interest in me for what it was worth, I had grown to be very suspicious of people who tried to impress me when I first met them. To be honest, this meeting would have meant more if Denise had just come alone and reintroduced herself. Maybe even explained where the hell she had been. But looking in her eyes, she seemed more caught up in her own reality, rather than paying attention to what I might feel or want. She might have money now, but she still didn't see who I was.

Four or five stores later we finally packed into the car. Little Richie seemed like he had too much for the day, because the car hadn't even started and he cuddled on the backseat ready to fall asleep. I kind of hoped he would stay awake. Maybe if I could interact with him I wouldn't have to participate in any unwanted conversation on the ride back. But poor little tired Richie was no help. He closed his eyes and there went my hope.

His dad broke the silence. "So Cindy, do you think you're ready for high school?"

Denise immediately interjected, "Of course she is. She's been the brightest of her class, honey."

Now the question that came to my mind was where had she gotten this information. For all she knew, I could have been a drop out. I never recalled her coming to check my report card. Did she have nerve or what? Was this yet another scene of imitating a real parent? Please, applaud the great show.

"Yeah, I'm ready," I replied.

"I hope so," Big Richie said.

Lucky for me the ride was short and they dropped me back to the Dawsons. My last weekend at what I called my home. With that thought alone, I felt like I could explode. I did not want to make this change. This ranked high on the worst changes of all. I decided to soak in all the love I could in the next forty-eight hours. I knew this sweet time was coming to an end, so I needed to just make the best of things. Let the good times roll once again.

It was a tearful goodbye that following Sunday, but the Dawsons made me promise to inform them on every detail of my first day of school. Before I walked out of the door I made sure I put on my most courageous and excited face for them. I didn't want them to worry about me, even though I knew they would. To see them so concerned with my happiness made my heart warm. They really did care for me. It just ended too soon for all of us.

I had to admit that Denise and Big Richie's home turned out to be a lot nicer than I imagined. A three bedroom apartment, fourth floor, clean hallways. Shocking. Even the inside of the apartment was cool. Blue and gray, blue and gray decorated everywhere. In every pattern from kitchen to bathroom. Couldn't say whether this was Denise's taste or not. I had never seen how she lived, only heard.

I had my own room. There wasn't much in there besides a high-rise bed and end table but hey, it was decent enough to be my new jail cell. I didn't think I would be spending too much time in there bonding, if you know what I mean.

Well, I started school from this place and whoa was high school rough. It was a fashion show to the third degree. I rode the bus, something I hardly had ever done alone and the city bus was a war zone for teenagers. The screaming, insulting, picking on other students. All happening in the back of the bus convinced me to hang near to the driver as often as possible.

Inside the school was no better. Academics was only a tenth as important as who liked who, or whose sneakers were the flyest. By the second week I guess you could say I found my clique or maybe to say my clique found me. My clothes helped a lot with that. As true as it was that I had never been big on image, it didn't hurt to be viewed as fly. Fly got me hanging with three girls: Shantell, Christine, and Tory. They all grew up together in the same neighborhood. Christine and Tory were sisters who had older siblings in their junior and senior year at the same school.

Shantell and I had no family to rely on for support and Shantell was definitely rough around the edges. She was cool, but had a reputation as a fighter that preceded her into high school. Even the teachers held her at a distance. She and I had most of our classes together so once we fell in I really didn't have to worry about trouble from any other students. The most trouble I worried about was from the teachers. No matter how many times a teacher told Shantell to stop talking to me in class, she just wouldn't. I know if my Nana were alive she might find fault with my new friends, especially with every other word out their mouths being vulgar. But I hoped that if she were here she would just understand. This was a jungle, and the life of a teenager.

School had become my getaway. Although I hated going home to the shady bunch I had no choice but to call my family, I had to keep going back. Still I kept my focus as much as I could. And for certain I kept my space. It took over three months for me to feel half at ease in that household. But eventually I stopped running to the Dawsons every weekend. Instead Denise encouraged me to hang more with the friends I had made. Some might think this was cool from a mother. But deep down I knew she was just jealous of Mrs. Dawson's relationship with me.

Still I liked this concern coming from Denise. Once she got the hint that smothering me wouldn't work, she started acting less annoying. In an attempt to be fair, I even quit being so hard on her. She was cool with me calling her Denise and I was cool with her trying to know me a little better. I couldn't tell you much about Big Richie though, he was gone quite a bit. When he was home he would always be with a bunch of men "talking business" as he would call it.

One night I strolled into the kitchen while they met around the table. I saw them dividing up what looked like thousands of dollars. Denise always stayed in the room with Little Richie, "Richie Boo" as I affectionately called him, while all this went on.

They watched me as I walked by them. Some cautiously, others provocatively. But without words Big Richie guided their attention back to work. I didn't know the nature of their business. But it didn't appear to be an honest one. Without needing a script, I knew the one part I had to play, and that was dumb and quiet! For playing this part, I earned jewelry, clothes, sneakers, you name it. It was a bargain I guess I was ok with keeping.

Every other weekend he sent me and Denise to the parlor as he hung out with Richie Boo. I have to admit, over a short amount of time, I became just as dumb and quiet as my mom was over this lifestyle. I have to say, Denise could sure pick' em.

During school, I had some picking to do of my own and the one I picked was Lavelle. His name should have been LOVE-velle, because he made me melt. Tall, handsome, brown eyes, Indian hair. He made wearing a high-top fade an art form. Even though he was one of the most popular boys in school, he didn't have a bad rep amongst the girls. Everyone liked him but he just kept cool. This made the hunt for his special attention even more intense.

I never thought I would be color struck. Especially after all the years of being called every monkey in the world, but light seemed right back then. Every girl checked for the light skinned boy, and Lovelle represented the epitome of that trend.

Listening to Shantell, Tory, and Christine boast about their experience with guys, I guess I began to get a little crazed myself. I was the only virgin amongst the crew and I anticipated changing that, especially if I had the chance with Lavelle. The girls made me feel like I was too old to be so inexperienced. I hid the fact that I had never even kissed a boy. They would have laughed at me. You never want to be the butt of their jokes. Peer pressure was brutal enough, but Shantell's mouth would have made it even worse.

I would hear Denise and Big Richie go at it some nights. Denise would scream sometimes as I heard Big Richie's heavy breathing. Hey I'm not proud of it but I imagined myself in Denise's place, consciously replacing Big Richie's face for Lavelle's. I had images in mind that were hard to shake. Watching things in movies that I probably shouldn't have didn't make it any better. Was it my fault that Richie didn't make hiding his personal movies a hunt? I could rewind them right back to where he left them and escaped all questioning.

Denise knew about Lavelle. She tried to give me wise words of precaution, but for the most part she gave me advice on how to make a boy pay attention to me. She told me one trick was to always stare at him until he notices, then turn away and act unenthused when he comes to make conversation. Not the rocket-scientist approach, but very effective as it turned out. Lavelle began to ask a lot of questions about me. He wanted to know where I was from, who I hung with and who was I dating.

It all kind of started after a cheap trick I learned off the television show, Happy Days. I dropped my bag "accidentally on purpose" so he could pick it up, and he did.

"Cindy Maze. That's your name isn't it?" he asked as he handed me the bag.

"How did you know?" I asked.

"I hear it twice a week in my favorite class. Study hall," he answered.

I smirked. "Study hall isn't a class silly."

He smiled back. "That's why it's my favorite." Before releasing the bag he asked, "Where you sitting?"

"Where I always sit." I finally got my bag from his grip.

"Well I don't know where that is, so I am asking."

"I sit at the right corner table next to the vendor machines with my girls."

"Oh, so you have friends?" he asked sarcastically.

"Yeah, what you mean by that question?" I asked with an attitude.

"You girls always calling these corny jealous chicks your friends, until they snatch your boyfriend."

"Well my girls ain't like that. I could trust them around my boyfriend."

"Do you even have a boyfriend?"

"What?" I answered smartly.

"I mean is there some boyfriend ready to get me for talking to his girl?"

"No, Lavelle," I answered.

"Lavelle? Oh so you do know who I am."

"Maybe. I mean, I know he knows he's fine. Who doesn't know his name?"

He smiled and said, "Well Cindy, I'm chilling with you. This might seem crazy to y'all but everybody's eyes seem to be on us and what were saying."

I could already see the burning in the eyes of the girls as we walked through the cafe.

"Uh huh look who C got tagging along!" Tory exclaimed as we got to the table.

"Yo this is LAVELLE," Shantell interrupted. "I know him. He's in my P.E. class."

I looked at Lavelle as his eyes began to roll the back of his head. "Shan- tell it all" he said. Mouth O Mighty, tongue everlasting.

"Who you talking about today?" LaVelle asked as Shantell sucked her teeth and turned her chair. Tory and Christine just stared at him.

"You sitting Lavelle?" Troy asked. He turned looked at me dauntingly and said "Naw I'm peace. See you another time Cindy." He got up and walked away.

I gathered that introducing him to the crew messed my whole game up, but still I sat trying to act nonchalant that my soon-to-be boyfriend just ditched me in front of my friends. But that's alright. That was only the first stage of my game. You see, my confidence had been boosted along with my butt and breasts. I was chocolate and cute, in a new territory with no old or bad memories. Everybody in this neighborhood knew "C" was no longer the hopeless, shifted-around, orphaned crack baby Cindy Maze.

I made my own name, getting more popular by the day. My tongue was getting sharper and my shyness was far behind me. If you didn't know better you would think I had turned into who Tanya used to be. Except I had no sister to cosign for me. I suppose the new me and the old Tanya would have gotten along just fine. Wow, what a difference a few months could make. I don't know the psychological reason for this change, but I bet my rebellion had some part in it.

As the school came towards an end, a lot changed in my life. I was the one now ranking on others. I gave my virginity to none other than LOVE-VELL. Popularity shot through the roof.

Back at the house, Big Richie stayed under me all the time. Denise started to act depressed and withdrawn, but me and Big Richie maintained a constant positive vibe. Matter of fact, Big Richie took me out by myself to the movies one Sunday, bonding I suppose, and Denise didn't seem so happy about it. Richie and I had fun out by ourselves. People of course stared at us, but I didn't care. I guess it did look sort of odd for me to be hanging with this obviously older man who looked nothing like a family member. But hey, I figured they were just jealous. Louis Vuitton clothes, matching mini-purse and red shoes. Everybody couldn't do it like this.

Of course, we laughed at how they were tripping. I mean there was nothing wrong with me and Richie hanging, was there? Besides, I thought, he feeds clothes and shelters me. We had a good ole time that night, then crept in with White Castle burgers around 11:30 pm. Denise was there at the door to angrily greet us.

"It's 11:30 and tomorrow is school. Why did you keep her out so late on a Sunday?" she yelled.

"Chill, Denise, stop flipping," he shot back.

She ranted and raved, until I knew it was getting too hot and heavy to stick around. I took my burgers into the room and closed my door slightly.

"Bitch," Richie shouted, followed by the sound of blows.

"Cindy!" Denise screamed.

I ran into their bedroom where she lay bleeding from the side of her left eye and mouth. I knelt to her side and helped her to use a t-shirt to wipe the blood. Her eye began to bulge.

Big Richie stood at the door holding Little Richie in his arm intensely crying from all the commotion.

"Look you woke up the baby acting like a crazy bitch," Big Richie shouted.

I looked at him bewildered, not really thinking if his hitting her was right or wrong. I never saw him lose his composure. Even though this was my mother, she taunted us and got on our nerves since we walked in. Still looking at Denise lay helplessly between her bed and the dresser, I felt her pains but said nothing.

Big Richie slammed the door shut and Denise looked me in the eyes.

"You don't go nowhere with that man without me. You hear me? You don't know him."

Her admonition confused me. How could she say I didn't t know him? I'd only lived in the same house with him the entire school year. Was she really worried or just jealous; scared we might go shopping or do something else without her? I was confused and jaded. But I held my tongue.

Between the last month of school and the events at home, change lingered thick in the air. A lot had happened during the spring, some of it for the worse rather than the better. One thing that went sour was our happy-go-lucky family. Big Richie and Denise went at it four nights a week, saying crazy, hateful things to each other. Denise looked like she'd lost fifteen pounds from stress, her skin blotchy from using foundation to cover all her newest bruises and cuts. I would catch her hollering at what appeared to be different females who would call at all hours of the night for Big Richie. I even heard her explode on him one night.

"Do what you want but if you fuck with mines, I'll kill you myself."

What was she talking about? What did she have that he threatened? Little had I known, but I was soon to find out.

One night I woke up early morning hours to go to the bathroom. With my eyes halfway closed and my nightcoat tied loosely, I opened the bathroom door and Big Richie stood there, naked, seeming to just have gotten out of the shower. I hurried to close the door back but he grabbed the knob from the other end and pulled the door back open even wider than originally, and just stood there looking at me with all his manliness exposed.

I walked backwards with both shock and fear at the fact he was, without words, telling me to explore his body. I turned the corner and walked back to my bedroom quietly and took my first breath as I closed my door and rushed under my cover.

"Whoa, what was that all about?" I asked myself. It was hard to block it out of my mind. Not only his body in fullness but the facial expression I'd never seen him display towards me. Talk about awkward, the morning sun that came too soon meant I would have to see Big Richie again, and worst of all: in front of my mother. How would he look at me? How could I look at him?

There was something deeply unsettling about undressing your mother's man with your eyes, intentionally or unintentionally. I wanted to act as normal as possible. Maybe Denise wouldn't notice the awkwardness that thickened the air? Maybe we could resume the normal life? Enough for wishful thinking, I thought, falling back sleep. Then to make matters worse, I lost track of time and overslept to 9:45.

No one bothered to wake me for school. I walked out of my room to the sound of Little Richie crushing his toy truck against the wall and the sound of the TV. I walked past Denise and Big Richie's room. Their door was open with no one inside. I continued on towards the living room ready for show time, but when I looked in there was just Big Richie and no Denise.

"Where's my mother?" I asked.

"Somewhere," he replied.

"Somewhere like where?" I asked again.

"She doesn't tell me what she's doing anymore. She just does it. I guess she meant for you to babysit because she knows I got things to do."

"Okay," I said and started to walk away.

"Come here," Big Richie said.

After a startled pause, I turned back around as he sat upward on the coach and patted the seat next to him. I didn't want to appear alarmed, besides at least he was dressed in a sweatsuit and socks. I walked over and sat. He looked towards the TV and asked, "How's everything in your world?"

"My world is cool, Richie"

He said, "Cool."

He then asked what my plans were for the summer. If I didn't know better, he almost sounded like a dad which, at this time, seemed pretty ironic. But still I answered, "I'm chilling this year."

"Dawsons?" he asked.

"I don't know," I answered back.

"Yeah I figure."

"You've gotten pretty advanced for chilling with the Dawson this year, huh?" he laughed smartly.

All the while I felt like there had to be something more behind his questions, and the fact that he didn't even bring up his being naked in front of me last night at all seemed real odd. I mean, he didn't forget and he knew I didn't either. So, what was up?

We said nothing. Richie Boo joined us on the coach and we sat staring at the TV for at least a good half an hour until the phone rang. Big Richie answered it and then went into his room. Soon after he returned dressed sharp like he worked on Wall Street, briefcase and all, and said "Don't go nowhere till your mom is back! Here is some money just in case you need it. And tell Denise I'll see her later."

He closed the door and I took my first real breath since I woke that morning. Little Richie Boo was well behaved as usual. Cartoons, cereal, and a nap, and he was good. But as for me, my mind wandered. Thoughts kept circling over and over in my mind. Should I tell Denise or not? It's not like he touched me or anything. I worried she might say I'm overreacting or, even worse, think I wanted to see him naked. With the two of them being on the edge, there was really no telling.

Finally at 3:30 p.m. I knew I would finally have somebody to talk to. School was out so I expected my peeps to come and check me with the gossip. Just as I suspected, the knock came. Shantell, came in and as tradition would have it she didn't say hi before she went straight to the gossip.

"Girl, did you miss it today. You know that girl Charlene the one with the big nose? Girl, she got her tail ripped by some chick.

I didn't even know she went to the school, and Terrance had some girl all wrapped up in the lunchroom. You know Tory was sick and…"

"Shantell, shut up," I interrupted."I got bigger drama."

"What kinda drama?" she asked.

"Big drama," I explained. "I saw Richie naked."

She looked over to Richie Boo sitting on the coach.

"No stupid. Richie" I said.

"Ooh girl, you freak."

"No Shantell, it was a mistake."

"Mistake my tail. How it looked?" she asked with a perverted expression.

"You are sick," I answered with a snappy attitude.

"Damn, Cindy, you act like you ain't never seen one before. Ain't they all the same?"

"No Shantell, never mind, Forget it," I said.

We paused then she spoke in a joking manner, "Next time you see it call me, I'll help you out!"

"You slut," I shot back laughing. "That's not funny!"

With this secret over my head, the following days had me on edge. Every look from my mother held suspicion, real or imagined. I watched my words carefully and noticeably kept my distance from Big Richie. I would only speak to him with my face turned elsewhere, trying to avoid too much contact. This helped to minimize how uncomfortable I felt with the whole situation. If no one else noticed, I knew for sure he did. The look on his face showed he didn't care one way or the other. . The tension between him and Denise had been frustrating for all of us. And the absence in Denise's eyes concerned me.

Finally we reached the end of the semester and my last report card was due at the end of the week. At last there was something besides this house to worry about. I just knew it was not going to be pleasing. Since the spring I had been pretty much lollygagging and acting a fool. I was more concerned about being the best dressed for the yearbook, rather than passing my classes or reading books. Books were not on my mind. I figured I would justify my failure by blaming the problems at home. But the truth was, I had been messing up long before. So what was my excuse? I had none! It reminded me of one of the only sassy thing I ever heard my Nana say, "Excuses are like butt holes, everyone's got one."

So much for Christian talk. Go Nana. Anyway, at this point I couldn't do anything about it, so why not worry about summer, I thought. Cute guys and short skirts. Before I knew it, the last day of school came. I had some overdue library fees but, surprisingly, the report card showed passing. I barely got by, but barely meant that I wouldn't get cussed by Denise.

On the way home from school I got my lies and explanations straight. I turned the key to my door, opened it and heard the television blasting. What's up with this? immediately came to mind. The living room was a mess, nothing like I had left it. It was sunny outside, yet the curtains were drawn shut. I felt something was completely odd about this whole scene. I dropped my bag to the floor, put my keys on the table and turned the television off. I began to place the pillows from off the floor back onto the couch. It didn't quite look like a break in, besides the door was locked. But like I said, something still felt odd.

A moment later, I heard what sounded like a rattling in the back of the apartment. As I got closer I recognized the sound of Richie Boo. I walked down the hall.

"Denise... Ma, where you at?" I called.

She didn't answer, but I heard LittleRichie begin to call my name. I walked past her bedroom but it seemed Little Richie was calling from way in back where my bedroom was. Richie Boo never went in my room without me. There was no way he could reach to unlock the door, so I knew immediately something was up.

I opened the door and saw Little Richie looking like he'd been crying for hours in his dirty Scooby Doo pajamas. I scooped him up into my arms as I turned on my lights and when I looked across my room, I felt like my heart could have popped out of my chest. Immediately, shock hit me. Little Richie began to cry even more as we stared at Denise laying nearly under my bed, seemingly unconscious.

I looked to the side of her and saw my vanity tray filled with stems, empty bags of whatever drug and a needle halfway pocked between her fingers. I didn't even move to touch her, I just took Richie ran to the living room phone to call the police. Just as I finished dialing, I heard Big Richie open the house door.

I didn't have a chance to tell my name to the operator before he screamed.

"What the hell!?!" The appearance of the house evidently had shocked him as well. "Cindy what's going on?" he shouted accusingly.

Between my own fright, the annoying operator, both Richie Boo and his father yelling, I naturally became very flustered. Big Richie didn't know who I was calling and ordered me to hang up the phone.

"But…" I stuttered.

"But nothing,"he said as he clicked the receiver.

"Denise probably dead in my room, she ain't moving or nothing," I said.

I could see the panic in his eyes as he turned and flew down the hallway toward my bedroom. I followed after him with Richie Boo in hand. I was really concerned about his reaction.

"Shit!" he yelled as he knelt to her. Richie pulled her upwards into his lap as she began making moaning sounds. He smacked her cheek repeatedly "Get up, wake up Denise. What's this shit?"

All she did was moan and nod, exposing the dried up tears that ran horizontal from her eyelids. I felt relieved to hear her respond, but she clearly was in a bad state.

"How long has she been like this?" he asked.

"I just got home"

"Where was Little Richie?"

"In here, sitting in the dark."

"This bitch," he scowled. "Richie, you okay?"

"Uh huh," Little Richie replied.

It was obvious that Richie Boo was still shook up. Who knows what he had to witness and for how long. It was needless to say this was not how I wanted to jump start my summer. But as crazy as my life had always been, I don't know why I was surprised. This was just a new entry in the crazy book.

Things went from bad to worse in the household at that point. For the three days that followed Denise just walked around in her housecoat and slippers drinking coffee. Big Richie had taken little Richie and been gone for two days, and I just didn't feel like going out, even with the weather being as beautiful as it was.

Denise tried to explain herself to me, but I was not ready to listen. It was all too much to finally witnessed the lifestyle that caused my world to be as chaotic as it had been since I was born. I preferred to have just imagined it in my mind, because reality hurt much worse.

I wondered when and how long she had been back into drugs, and if was this the reason for her being absent lately. However, my deepest concern was how were things going to be when Richie got back. Was he just going to leave us or kick us out? What was going to happen now? Once again Denise was destroying everything for me. I couldn't believe I was worried about being embarrassed by my report card, when she was hiding her drug abuse.

Well anyways, my mind and emotions kept me on the edge. I kept thinking if anything happened, where would I go? Hopefully back to the Dawsons, but since I hadn't been keeping too much contact with them lately I doubted the likeliness of this. I was scared, and I knew I had good reason to be.

I raged in silence until the afternoon Big and Little Richie returned. At this time Denise had been staying in my room since she'd been locked out of her own, and I was just lounging on the couch.

Richie asked immediately, "Where is your mom?"

"In the room," I answered.

He said "Oh" as he looked towards the back.

"Put these groceries up," he said as he placed four bags on the table.

Little Richie had already begun digging through them to get himself cookies, and for the first time in awhile I looked Big Richie in the eyes. "How are you doing?" I asked.

He looked back at me but gave no response. This to me said a lot.

During this awkward interaction we could hear Denise coming out the room. I guess the sight of Richie made her turn back, and I couldn't blame her. I put away the groceries while interacting with Little Richie. But I had noticed the fact that he hadn't asked where his mother was. And for a moment I think neither him nor I cared. I did everything to put the worry behind in my thoughts, but I knew eventually something big was going to happen, and soon.

Good or bad, I just felt it was inevitable that something would be changing around here. But ironically, within the couple of days that followed, there was a strange peace that came over the home. Richie and Denise finally began to exchange words. Not many, but enough to appear cordial. This came with a lot of help from Little Richie. I must say Richie Boo was smart for his age. It's like he had masterminded a way to get both Richie and Denise's attention at the same time. Even his silliness paid off with laughter.

I admired his intentions but my suspicious nature awaited an explosion and I just wanted to be clear of it. It was either true love that Big Richie and Denise shared, or a perfect charade. I was betting on the charade option. Love has too many layers for me, and if

I knew nothing more, I knew everybody had a different definition of it. I have heard the saying, "I love you" said by too many. But I know I have only felt it once, and that was from Nana. I really don't know what it was that the two of them shared but I was soon to discover more than I wanted.

WHEN IT HIT THE FAN

Summer resumed. I had to get my mind off what had been going on, so my first line of defense was my homegirls. I had completely ignored them for the past few days. I made the phone call. Where? When? Who? I got all the details and I was out the door. Finally out of the hibernation, I figured all would be well enough without my monitoring.

What I needed to monitor more than Denise and Big Richie was what was up with Lovelle. I hadn't heard from him since the last day of school and my stubbornness would not let me call him first. I just wanted to see how long I had to be unheard from before he checked on me. I already had rehearsed the whole speech I was going to give him once he tried to reach out. But meanwhile, it was time to catch up with the girls. If anyone could give me a rundown on what I missed, it was going to be Shantell.

And just as I had assumed, no time was wasted before I was privy to every scandalous detail of the whole neighborhood's life. Including Lovelle's whereabouts.

Getting the whole gossip from Shantell, it seemed like a year worth of drama that I had missed. I heard about some of the house parties that had gone on. Especially the ones Lovelle had visited. Of course, without me asking anything specific, Shantell offered up all the details. She told me what he was up to, who he danced with, who was checking him out and most importantly if he asked about me. When she said that he had, though I didn't want to seem too excited, inside I jumped for joy thinking I've gotta give him a call tonight.

Anyways, we walked the sunny blocks, sat in the basketball courts and finally went to Christine's house and sat on the porch. It wasn't long before we had a lot of company. Guys from off her block crowded us, curious of who me and Shantell were. Although, neither of them were my type because Lovelle was my only type, I entertained their flirting and compliments. Shantell did the same, but with the difference of her faithfully sassy attitude. I mean, she can turn anything into an argument in a moment flat. I had gotten really good at explaining to others what I thought she had really meant. Especially when the guys would say to me "You are pretty to be dark-skinned." Although in some warped way they may have meant it as a compliment, Shantell hurried to my defense saying, "Just say she pretty then leave her alone. She ain't interested!" Her snazzy remarks saved me mine. So I guess having this type of friend paid off.

Just like any and every conversation around boys, the conversation was about sex. I usually hated this line of talk, because somehow it would end up with someone telling too much information about the other. Soon after there would be competition or an argument. It truly never failed. Even though I tried to stay out of it, somehow without me opening my mouth, I would get added into the conversation, usually starting with the statement, "Don't act all innocent C. You know you ain't no virgin!"

Sometimes I would snap at my defense, but today after all I had going on at home, I just decided to giggle it away. I just needed to be a part of the normal nothingness.

After a while the dimness of the afternoon became my excuse to be on my way. "I have something to check on. I'm about to be out." I announced. I saw the curiosity in the girls eyes as they knew I was never the first to want to go home. Still I gave them all the I'm cool look and said, "Check y'all later."

I left them and walked far out of my way. Just needed some me time I suppose. But as I heard people say before, everything happens for a reason. Along my detour was a bus stop. And standing at it was my cousin Dessa, looking less like herself than I had remembered.

"Cuz, what's up? I asked as she hesitatingly turned my direction.

"Cindy, what you doing over here?"

"Know some people over here," I responded.

"Where you coming from?"

"Just visiting somebody, but I gotta get home."

"Yeah what's up with everybody? I haven't heard from y'all since you know..?"

"Yea I know, but everybody just coping. Talking about moving to Georgia for a minute."

"Georgia?" I asked."That's far."

"I know." Dessa said. "But hey."

Dessa's facial expression drop along with her eyes. I knew why they would be thinking about moving. Tanya being gone must have made it difficult staying in the old neighborhood. It was random seeing her at this bus stop, but I knew it was no time for me to really get in her head or her into mine. I just told her to maintain. I gave her a hug with a promise I would visit.

Seeing Dessa left me with a strange feeling, even about my own situation. I wished we were close enough to confide in each other, being family and all. But the truth was that things had changed. How much? I just didn't know. I might have even still been the subject of ridicule in that household, but I really couldn't say I cared anymore.

I decided to cut my adventure short as the darkness fell. I headed home, walked in the house to see Richie Boo laid out on the couch. His toys were everywhere but I didn't see anyone else until I walked towards the back rooms. There, through the crack of their door I saw my mom and Big Richie laid in the bed and it looked like they were cuddling.

"That's you Cindy?"Denise called out.

"Yeah, It's me," I replied.

"I'll be in the back."

I walked to my room a little relieved to see them together, and in that way: tenderly. But not relieved enough to forget to be suspicious. I mean, it just doesn't happen that way, where all is forgiven so quickly. What was the penalty for the last week? I refused to believe there was none. Then again, what did I know? Maybe things work this way, and I just never gave them a chance. Worry would just have to wait until the morning I thought there was nothing I could have done about it any how.

THE LONG AWAITED

I slept until the early afternoon the next day. The benefit of it being summer was the lively music playing in the house. The smell of breakfast still lingering despite the hour. I anticipated a fine breakfast but all that remained was a piece of bacon and cold eggs. I guess it was going to be cereal and milk for me after all. Big Richie sat in the kitchen with the sunlight beaming off his well-shined face.

"Cindy what brings you to join the land of living?" he jokingly asked.

"I was tired, Richie, couldn't help it. Where's my mom and Boo-Boo?"

"Gone like you about to be" he said with an unreadable expression.

My heart skipped beat momentarily and seriousness came into my eyes. "What you mean?"

"Nothing, your mom's handling things but I need you to do something for me a little later. Is that fine?"

I sighed in relief, happy to have misunderstood so I answered "yes" without even questioning what it was that he wanted from me. I mean whatever it was, it had to be better than what I thought, right?

I ate my breakfast, dangled around for an hour or more than decided to get dressed for the day. By this time I was dressed and made a few phone calls. Big Richie was dressed also and having what sounded like a regular phone call. I walked into the living room where he stood as he told whomever he was speaking to that he would call them back.

"Good. You are dressed. I need you to do something for me."

I nodded my OK as I sat on the couch and waited for my assignment. He went into his room, came out holding what seemed to be a letter and a backpack. Seeing the envelope, I naturally expected he wanted me to go to the post office, but the book bag confused me.

Big Richie asked me to have a seat. Which seemed really odd since I was already sitting. There came that strange feeling again. He rubbed my shoulders and patted my hair before he sat beside me.

"Cindy, it's important what I need you to do. You know Perry, the big ugly dude that is here sometimes with me?"

"Yeah," I responded.

"I need you to drop something to some of his people. I'm going to put you in the cab so don't worry about where you need to go. Just give the guy at this address this bag. It might seem a little heavy, but you can handle it. After, I want you to give him this envelope. He will tell you what to do next. Alright?"

I looked at Big Richie with silence as he gave his instructions, but for whatever reason it seemed like he had a problem talking and looking me in the eyes.

I used to hear Nana talk about the exact thing I was experiencing with Big Richie. It was something like "The devil can't stand the light, so he hides his face." Silly I guess in words, but in context she always told me to talk with people straight up. Always look people directly in the eyes, because that's where a person's truth and intent lie.

I think I understand that now, but of course I didn't really get it then. Nana used to always talk over my head, but I didn't have a problem remembering everything the way she said it. For some strange reason, I felt the need to remember that lesson about the devil now. Still I dismissed the thought considering that Big Richie had never asked me to do anything for him before. And after this crazy week, I felt honored he would want my help. Besides, as much as he has done for us, it might have been disrespectful to decline this errand. I figured he must just be busy or else he would have done it himself, right? I put my smile on.

"OK, Richie it'll cost some new sneakers though," I said to lighten the air. We both laughed.

He dialed the car service as I fixed my hair and checked myself in the mirror. I was secretly making my plans for the day: drop this package off for Big Richie and then go find Lovelle. That was a smooth plan for my afternoon.

The honk downstairs meant it was time to go. I went to pick up what was a heavy book bag and unlocked to leave the door.

"And oh Cindy, don't be nosey and open that bag. Don't want nothing to fall out."

"OK," I said, walking out the door.

I was halfway down the stairs when I heard Big Richie running after me, muttering "Oh, oh I gotta pay the cab for you." He ran quickly past me, and by the time I walked out the building he was already backing away from the cab.

"I told him where to take you. I paid him already, you cool?"

I jumped in the cab, "Later Richie."

SOLD

The driver hardly spoke a lick of English and played Spanish tunes the whole ride. The heat of the leather seats burned my body and the windows only went down half way, irritating me till no end. I observed the fact that we jumped on the highway, and then I began to think:hey I didn't sign up to be on no field trip! We must have been driving for a good hour by now and my head was hurting from the heat and the noise of his terrible music. Finally we approached a kind of neighborhood that didn't look like any place anyone would want to be. It was torn down.

"Are you at the right place, Papi?"

"Yeah yeah, Tu padre said here, I got it, I got it."

I sat back as we circled these crippled blocks where it seemed like a bunch of alcoholic and dope fiends had taken over. Didn't see much but skinny ladies with unmatched outfits and do-rags tied on their heads until the car stopped.

"OK OK," the driver said.

I looked on the envelope which read Sargent 553. I looked out the window at the dilapidated brownstone in front of me. 553.

"Alright Papi wait here."

"Where you going?"he asked.

"I just have to drop this off. Then you'll take me back to where you picked me up?"

"Pay now Bonita, pay now?"

"Wait. Papi, chill. My pops will pay when we get back. This will only be a minute."

I opened the door as he gave me the "I don't know look" and I asked, "Are we cool?"

He looked back as I stepped out with the bag, and as soon as I shut the door he zoomed off.

"That crazy mother..." I grunted. Well, I thought, there's nothing I could do about him now. I just needed to drop this off and get the hell on my way. This was New York, a couple of cents on the bus or train I'd be OK.

I opened a dragging gate and went towards the downstairs door. I knocked, trying not to get the dirt of the door all over my hands. No answer. I knocked on the window next to it, loud and impatient. A minute later I heard someone with an attitude yell "Wait!" I couldn't believe whoever it was had the nerve to be annoyed. They should have a bell. I then heard someone coming. Click, click, click, click.

What the hell? I was thinking to myself. How many locks they got on this door? Who gone break in this shack?

A big guy opens the door and says simply: "Come." I hesitated but I entered. He walked me into the hallway, opened another door which seemed to get me into the living area of this place and before I knew it I was standing at the threshold of a smoke-filled room with faces I couldn't really make out. It was dim and dingy, and I really wanted to make this whole exchange go quick, so I asked, "Who's Sargent?"

Another big guy walked in from what seemed like a kitchen and said "That's' me. Who's asking?" He walked toward me and just grabbed the book bag. "Come," he said. Talk about rude. All my alarms went off at this point. I still I followed this man deeper into the house. He opened some double door to what seemed like a more livable part of this house.

"Richie," he said.

"Yes," I replied.

He pointed me to sit down. We sat on the couch and he threw the book bag on the table, "Oh and here." I passed him the envelope. He put the envelope to the side and opened the backpack in front of me.

He pulled out at least twenty sandwich bags of this white powder. That's when my eyes popped. I couldn't believe what I was looking at.

"Rasclot," he said strongly as he inhaled what smelled like Marijuana.

I read his expression as I could tell he was pissed. He opened the letter as I now sat as close to the edge of this couch as I could. My body tightened as I began sweating from fear. He read the letter to himself, threw it on the table and leaned back on the couch puffing and steering at the ceiling. I was curious to what this letter could possibly say, what it was that had him smacking his teeth in disgust. He looked feverishly toward me and after a moment of silence he screamed, "Claudie, Disa one Ere!"

I looked to see who he may have been calling and why. That's when another big body entered the room, this time a woman. She wasn't near pretty at all. She had to be about 300 pounds and about 6 feet tall. Her breasts alone, were the size of submarines. Her manly features and greasy neck now approached me and started yanking at me.

"What's up? What's going on?" I yelled. At my every plea this woman tightened her grip, pulling my arms. "What's wrong?" I continued to yell as my eyes now began to well up from pain and fear and confusion.

"Come now gal," she muttered through our scuffling.

By now all the fight I had in me surfaced. My fear had escalated to panic as I was confused to why I was here and now seemingly being detained. I thought of all the threats and curse words I could muster, hoping she would tire from my resistance and let me go. But instead this woman just tightened her hold. She wrapped around my torso strongly, seeming to be unaffected by my kicking and screaming. All the while Sargent sat coolly on the couch, facial expression unchanging, smoking as if I weren't crying for my life. Then he suddenly walked up to us and with his right hand extended, grabbed me by the neck forcibly and said, "Looka here Yute. You fuss we hurt you, you scream we shoot you, you try and run we slaughter you. Fuck up and obey what me a say. Alright?"

At this point it became all too real to me. I knew from the terror this man spoke without a flinch of human remorse, I was not leaving. I let it settle in my body that this was another beginning of another terrible story of my life. I had no choice but to ease my fight and be escorted to a dark and cool basement. As far I could see a bunch of corroded mattress with everything pissy to fishy you could smell were laid on the floor. Certainly, this was the worst sleeping arrangement I've ever had and I've have plenty. My mind sat in this place investigating it and plotting my escape. I didn't want to move too hastily through. I understood it was going to take some time, but I would get away from here.

By now the pressure I felt had reached the level to have an anxiety attack. But I've always known to try to keep some degree of cool in dramatic situations. Or at least I heard that you should. But who could have thought I would be here? I didn't. A forced thought of optimism came to my mind. Maybe they're just holding me shortly. Big Richie knows where I'm at. Surely, after a while he would have to be concerned why I hadn't returned. If not him, Denise would surely check for me after a while. I sat pondering these thoughts as I twiddled my fingers and tried to tame the uncontrollable trembles of my body. Calm down, Cindy I repeated over and over in my head. Calm down!

I sat quietly listening to the footsteps from above, hoping anyone would come and unlock this door and let me go. It seemed like forever in time before I heard the lock click open. I jumped up "Hello please can I leave? It's getting really late now," I said in my most innocent of tones, to only be ignored.

A woman walked past me as if I weren't even there, grabbed something, walked up the stairs and locked the door again behind her. Now worry really began in full bloom. Stupid me! Trying to reason with these animals. I should have just ran up them stairs and busted out while I had the chance. This can't be for real, I said to myself. It just couldn't!

I sat on the bed as I presumed the night changed into morning. I don't recall closing my eyes; not once. I had ignored my needs to eat and to use the bathroom. These people never even checked on me to eat or go to the bathroom. How wicked could they be? I thought. How wicked.

I sat so long with not much to look at the smells started becoming normal by this point. My eyes burned and my head ached. I couldn't fight it anymore. I leaned my head against the cement wall and I nodded off. For a brief moment, I wasn't there anymore. I was in my home in my bed even hearing the chuckles of Richie Boo in my ears. As a flash in my dreams I imagined hearing Big Richie and Denise saying, "Cindy get up! we are leaving here." But this refuge of slumber didn't last for long.

"Wake up pissy gal, wake up!" I was pulled out of my dream by the big bruno woman.

"Let's go," she said.

I shook my head as it seemed I was in some kind of twilight. I felt weak and soaked in my own urine. I can't believe I peed myself. I hadn't done that since who knows when. I walked up the stairs after her. They're letting me go, I thought. Thank God! But apparently my gratitude came too soon. She gave me a plastic bag with what seem like clothes and told me I was going in the van outside.

"Van," I said. "Why? Where? Am I going home?"

She just looked at me as to not even dignify me with a response. She gave me a small container of what look like rice and peas with some meat and said, "Go on girl, and don't think of getting smart out there." Could this be a word of concern or was it a threat? I was too weak to judge. I did as she said and walked out the front door.

It was nighttime. Hot and humid, but surely a different day. The block was isolated so there was no sense in screaming or fussing. Crack heads were not likely to jump out of hiding and save the day, I thought. I made the decision to just do what I had to do. Survival I was concerned with. Remaining as long as I could outside of that basement was my goal. I had a better chance of getting away I figured, if I thought smart. The obviousness that Big Richie hadn't come for me left me even more concerned. How could he? What did I do to him? And has he done with my mom and brother?

A lot of things raced through your mind in panic. Even while sitting in this van that looked too beat up to be on the road, I caught different glimpses in my mind of how to get out of this situation. I remembered someone coming to my school about a year ago talking about fires, kidnapping, and other emergency situations. Had I known that this could actually have happened to me, I mean, really happen to me; I would have paid closer attention.

It wasn't until the whole ordeal with Tanya did it even strike me as real or a possibility for anyone. I wondered if this was some kind of karma coming to haunt me. I mean, did I not grieve correctly over Tanya? Was there something else? Some sign I had missed? I already thought my life was unfortunate. All I really needed was to figure out where I was going, and why.

Curtain material draped tightly to the side window made attracting attention from oncoming traffic impossible. I contemplated climbing backward over the seats, and out of the back doors, but I knew it wouldn't be easy. Especially since the passenger kept his eyes fixed on my every move. My second strategy was to play the pleasant role. Maybe my lack of fight and fear in my eyes would bother their conscious and they'd just let me go. So I worked my innocence the best I knew how. And while even doing so, it seemed neither of them cared a bit.

The life of Cindy Maze is never boring I suppose.

Subconsciously, I counted the lights we passed until it seemed we were on the highway. I figured I would try to measure how far out they were really taking me. A hour passed until we made our first stop. The van parked off at a dimly-lit gas station.

The driver stepped out of the van and shortly after I noticed what seemed like car lights from a different vehicle. This car had come to a halt right beside us. I sat quietly to listen to the voices. I heard the voices of the two other men talking to the man who drove the van I was in. I didn't understand what they were saying clearly since they all carried such a heavy accent. Soon after the doors to my van opened and the three men stood looking at me. The heavyset man spoke "She good! Bring her."

"Bring me? Where?" I didn't know why but I just gave my face of confusion as I was ordered out of the van. Just then tears automatically fell from my eyes, one after another until instantly it seemed I would dissolve in them. And just like that I was traded like an animal. Where I ended up was somewhere in the Midwest in a prostitute rink with other young girls such as myself.

I still can remember my first night with a John. A man who looked like he could have been one of my high school teachers, entered the motel room. He was a white male that was medium built and wore glasses. At first I thought he might be a sensible man that I could explain how I had been abducted. Maybe he would feel sorry that I was so young and only there against my will. Instead, he sat on the end of the bed, looking quiet and humble in the face. His eyes seemed empathetic until he stood up, unzipped his pants and called me over to him. At first I thought that with his subtle demeanor I could still do my convincing with tears streaming from my eyes, but I could see the sight of my terror was making him aroused. As if another man had been hiding inside of him, he advanced boldly toward me and grabbed me by my neck. He pushed all his weight onto my shoulders until he had me postured on my knees facing only his nakedness. Using the strength he had as an advantage, he turned what some may consider foreplay into war-play. What was left of my innocence or naivete was taken at an instant. After he had done what he had wished with me, he passed word to our pimp that I was unsatisfying. He told him how I complained and tried to talk him into helping me get away.

Later that night my capture brutally raped me. He scorned me with his words and threatened if I had ever tried that again he would kill me. He pounded himself into me until I vomited from the unbearable pain. He released himself inside of me and and all I could hear were his terrifying moans and feel of his hairy body crushing me beneath him. Eventually he got up. I laid broken on my stomach, face smeared in my own fluids. My throat burning from my violent screams a lingering thought that I wanted to die right at that moment. He promised he would do it again until I loved it.

In the following weeks he tried to break me like a horse in the stable. But it wasn't just me alone I noticed. One of the girls that shared my fate was pregnant when she was abducted. I heard he was the one that beat her until she miscarried.

This was hell. He was Satan. I was scared! But before I knew I was sold again.

I tried my best with the new rink to be compliant. They were already weary of me after being told I was a talker. But the truth was, I was no longer a talker, I was a zombie. These people offered the girls liquor, weed, cocaine. They kept us all high off of something. You either took it voluntarily or a substance would involuntarily be shot through your veins. I guess they wanted us so messed up that we couldn't escape. Some of the ones who'd been there longer were so addicted that their addiction kept them unwilling to leave. Drugs were made to mean more than freedom.

I had managed to make them believe that weed and alcohol was so powerful toward my system that I didn't need anything else. Truth is, though I looked sedated, I still maintained some sort of awareness. I just never let on. I needed them to forget to be leery of me. I survived months without scars until I was traded again. This time it was to a bigger city. I learned the corner at this time. For the first time I not only feared my captures but I had to watch the girls also.

Everybody wasn't on these corners with the same conditions. Some were so gone they had rationalized this lifestyle and actually found pride in catching Johns. It was not abnormal to see a cat fight or two over something petty. It was an adapted mindset of a zoo. Cops would come and sweep girls up few by few. But a week later they were back. I used to pray a cop tried to pick me up. But I was never so lucky. Besides my captures never stayed less than an ear shot away. Most Johns were handled parked in a alley. I felt hopeless.

But it eventually came the time that fear had turned to anger and anger into fight. I preferred that they would kill me before I killed myself. And I remember the night I was ready to commit suicide by murder. It was either that or escape. But I knew escape was the lesser of the possibilities. I drugged myself into painlessness and I went for the kill. The ultimate revolt arrived when I came against my capture with a blade I had found on the streets one day. I had held on this blade for a while deciding if I would use it toward myself or someone else. Hearing my Nana's voice in my ears saying this body you used was borrowed. It belongs to God, and to harm it was Sin. And while Sin didn't scare me anymore, I feared I would only be trading one hell for another.

He came into my room and I charged him. I felt the blade enter the flesh of his neck, but I didn't do the damage I had hoped, because in my next memory the pattern of the bed spread danced to the awkward rhythm of my heart. My eyes burned from the combination of sweat, dirt and tears and my face went between numbness and a stinging pain. I struggled to lift myself up, but my body resisted. How long had I laid here with dry blood on my arms and chest? My eyes searched the room in a blur.

Take five minutes Cindy, I said to myself. I closed my eyes and spoke to my body from within. My legs began to tingle and I felt a cool sensation travel from my toes up to my thighs. I was naked and if I had the strength I would have covered myself to avoid this chill. But I knew to try to relax was my best solution.

I needed to become more alert but the more I tried the more I felt myself slipping into daze. It felt like being awake watching myself sleep. I knew I needed to get up.

But how was the question.

I suppose I was no help to myself because the next time my eyes opened I saw a stream of light peep from the sides of the drapery. There was sun on the other side of that window, and all I wanted was to feel the intense rays warming my skin.

Enough time must have passed because I felt it was a little easier to move my body. I took my first pull of strength to roll over onto my side. With another tug I flipped myself over into my stomach and paused for a deep breath. I heard the crackling of my shoulders as I pushed myself upward from the bed until I was sitting in a praying position. I should have stayed that way for longer, because when the time came to lift my head, I felt a rumbling and pounding thump like I have never felt in my life.

"Awhh," I sighed, as I was made aware of every bruise, tear and cut.

Why did I feel like I was ran over by a bus? Better yet, why did I look like I did?

My nose locked in to the strong aroma of filth and urine and cigar. And then it all came back to me. This is where I had experience the worst pit of assault in my life.

I have got to get away, and now! Before someone comes back to get me.

I looked around the room and remembered just where I was. There was only one question: how could I escape?

With energy, adrenaline and panic I slid myself off the bed, picked up the dress that lay right at the foot of the bed and limped into the bathroom. I caught a glimpse in the mirror of the terror that had become me. And though I looked nearly unrecognizable from the outside, the Cindy inside knew that this was my chance to escape.

Quick rationalizing…. leaving out the front door will not work.

I climbed on the ledge of the tub and slid a small rusty window open. From it I could see cars racing down the street. At a distant gate I saw two homeless ladies sitting on what look like crates next to a shopping cart mounted with tons of stuff. A jump from this second level, would be difficult. I looked back around the bathroom to see if there would be something that would aid me, but all that lay was a small bath towel a roll of toilet tissue a little cup. Dammit, why couldn't this place have bath curtains instead of these filthy smudged glass doors? Hopelessness snuck its way into my heart as my mind told me to accept my defeat.

After a short pause, I reconsidered. I had no choice. Either I take this short fall, pick myself and run, or stay and let these people continue to beat me near death. Just when I became totally convinced I would take the jump I heard the sounds of men talking in the room.

"Yo, where is she?"

"She was right here Man, nobody moved her."

I heard a man's voice grunt angrily in the background as I was now edging the walls with my feet. I was using all the upper body strength I could muster to try and lift me into this small window.

But it was too late. A strong arm pulled my body backward

into his tight grip. I let out a screeching plea, "Let me go, please just let me go!"

But these men were just bodies. Their eyes were cold and tense. And never did they flinch in remorse.

My mind skips on some of the things that happened next. But I guess I remembered what they wanted me to remember. And that was that. There was no getting away, at least not alive.

A few weeks had passed and I had somewhat recovered from my bruises. But fear still stained my memories. I only saw blurred visions of my past. The Cindy that could have fought back was gone. I had checked absent in so many ways that my mind had gone somewhere else and wasn't fighting to find me. My soul sat on the side of my body watching these men mount my flesh.

This is how I remember emptiness.

I was made a prisoner in that room for weeks, with Johns being my only other human contact. I looked so bad that I knew they only had to be charging half-price for me. Even when I began to look normal, I didn't feel it. People have no idea what goes on in the dark gutters of the world, I now do. First thing to go is your ID, then your hopes, and afterward it seems your mind.

The scars and wounds on my body healed but my nightmares became brutal. It became harder to remember the happier times when I was s child. Because those memories were even mixed with difficult times. I had to question what part of my life I would have wanted to relive, and all I could think about was the Maze home. But I was giving up on hope. Hope gave me black eyes and fractured ribs. I just couldn't imagine having fight in me anymore. I was overpowered and out willed. The Cindy from before was no more.

I turned eighteen in a dirty motel after my last trick. Needless to say, it was not the best way to turn into a woman, but I dealt with the cards handed. For the last year although everything about this lifestyle stunk, it seemed I had lucked out just a bit. I was traded into a halfway decent rink. Saying this might sound bizarre, but considering the options this was something to be grateful for. Fear is the whip that kept us girls in order, but these guys who had us were young. Although they were still intimidating, they used the psychology of acting as protectors to keep order.

In this new rink, you would hardly hear of anyone being disciplined. Girls being harmed by tricks or what they'd like to refer to as clients was not tolerated. We were treated as product marketed and sold to the highest bidders. In other words, these Johns took baths{lol}. They seemed like men that maybe even had a profession or family at home.

A guy called P.R. controlled this prostitution rink. I don't figure this was his real name, but I know I overheard his partner call him Parker. He looked at least 27 or 28 years old., more clean cut then what I've dealt with in the past and a lot more articulate than his other partners. Parker had this air about him that made me and some of the other girls think he really cared. But if you looked closely you could see the kill in his eyes. But had he ever actually killed anyone? It would be hard to tell.

"Treasure" was the name I was given by this life. One of my early captors who put his gun to my lips on many occasions started calling me this. Since I had never given my real name to anyone and didn't intend to, I let them refer to me as they wished.

I remember at least a month into me being picked up by these guys, another girl who had been under Parker and his set for a while befriended me. In one of our conversations she told me if I acted right and did what I was told I might have a chance at being released. She said that she'd witnessed it happen to another girl when she first arrived.

Of course this all seemed crazy to me. I asked her if the girl was just traded. She said no they let her go by herself. Though it hardly seemed possible because nobody was here under their own free will. This gave me just a glimpse of hope. Still I questioned, if that were the case, why hadn't she been set free. Although it was at the edge of my tongue, I chose not to ask this question in fear that she might be offended. I really appreciated having someone to talk with and I didn't want her to become uncomfortable in any way.

Despite what on the outset could seem outlandish, some of what she told me seemed a bit possible. I knew that prior to being under Parker, girls weren't even allowed to go to the store or communicate with any of the outside world. Oftentimes you were blindfolded, transported and stuck in a motel room for months at a time. Rarely. if ever, venturing further than the car lot or being able to speak to one another. Amazing how we were all steps away from each other with usually just a wall between us yet we didn't even know each other's name.

Things were slightly different under Parker. After the initial or subliminal threats, we were granted a limited feeling of freedom. Not enough freedom to open up to a stranger to get help, because that was still committing suicide. But it felt better to walk a tightrope than have one around our necks. Feminine products were given monthly, something I had never experienced before in captivity. Something so simple as a scented bar of soap felt like a luxury. Something to carve your name into, and for a temporary time, have ownership over. Of course it wasn't just given as a pleasantry. Likely it was equivalent to washing a car before it's sold, But it felt good.

Some might ask with all this freedom why didn't I try to get away but to that I say, sure as hell was evident there were no search parties sent out to find me. Trying to alert authorities or anyone else could have you wrapped in a plastic bag under a bridge. At the very least, some who have attempted escape ended up with their teeth knocked out. And guess what? The tooth fairy stays far away from the dark corners we lived on. I handled myself to survive. I prayed often that opportunity would present itself to get away. My Nana used to sing a song that said, "The lord would make a way somehow"so I figured all I had to do was wait on my somehow.

If there was nothing else I knew for sure, I knew that I was becoming stronger. Not quite in the physical since, but in my mind. I watched girls being taken out in the depths of night, because they had taken their own lives. Some used drugs until their limbs could move but their minds went nowhere. Gratefully, that wasn't me.

Luckily drugs didn't take to my system in a habit-forming way. I had already seen the worst of what it could do, and the last thing I ever wanted to be was like my mother. I began to remember more about who Cindy Maze was. The Cindy that was popular in school. The Cindy that had the cutest boy as her beau. Most importantly, I was a big sister to the most adorable little boy in the world.

It killed me to not know what was going on with Richie Boo, but it stayed my motivation. If he were in harm's way, which was totally likely, I knew that he needed me. So even after the many nights of crying, I knew I could not give up. If not for my sake, but for his.

PERFECT TIMING!

Talk about being in the right place at the right time. I walked into what seemed like a heated discussion between Parker and his other partners in the ring. As soon as I walked into their sight Parker said "And her too." My eyes said, "Me? What?" but I kept my lips shut. I didn't remember doing anything wrong, so I didn't know whether to panic or not. I worked on limiting my worries as I tried to understand what was going on. A couple of more heated words later between them, I was told by Faze, the older and more aggressive of the partners, to go get my stuff and leave with Parker.

Parker interrupted saying, "Just give me what's mine, and she can leave all that shit she has here."

I stood confused, yet anxious. If I were hearing correctly, I was leaving. To where I didn't know, yet I found myself standing patiently behind Parker awaiting their resolution. Parker turned to me and said "Go wait in my car. As a matter of fact, get the two girls in the room next to you and you all go wait in my car." His instructions sounded urgent, so I turned quickly in compliance. "Tell them to leave their junk!" he yelled as I walked away. As the door closed, I heard the men threaten that if Parker left, he was declaring war. But Parker never gave a response of fear.

Of course I was met with a million and one questions by the girls when I knocked on their door. I couldn't answer any of them, but just as I had known, they had also known also to just do as they were told. We all went and sat in the car. Moments after the girl that I would speak to sometimes walked onto the balcony of the motel. Her hands motioned in a way to be asking me what was going on. Where were we going? I signaled my hands to let her know I didn't know. She stood staring at the car in her yellow mini dress, with eyes like a child who was being left behind.

Shortly after this exchange, Parker stormed out of one of the motel rooms with two large evening bags. I watched him look up at the woman on the balcony, but he just continued to walk toward the car. Although I had no idea where he was taking us, I sort of wished he would signal for her to come too. Who knows, I may have been on my way to doom, but atleast I had the fortune of my imagination. I already knew for certain who she would be left to deal with. It just wasn't a pleasant thought.

Parker put his bags in the trunk, jumped in the driver's seat and zoomed through and out of the parking lot. We held on to our seats tightly. I figured there was no time for asking questions when he's driving like a mad man. Fifteen minutes into this rollercoaster we pull up at a diner. He told us to get out, we were going inside.

We all walked into the diner. With everybody in their work clothes, we stuck out like a sore thumb. It's such a surreal feeling being an outsider to what is normal. You always wonder if anyone could see your pain. And if they could, would they do anything about it?

We had no choice but to ignore the attention as we were escorted to a bench table in the far corner. When we were given a menu. I crammed my face deeply into it trying to avoid my own curiosity and big mouth. Someone would have to ask what's going on but it wasn't gonna be me. I had never witnessed Parker being so upset and frustrated. I didn't know to what capacity it would affect me, so I chose to keep my silence. Luckily before my patience expired, the silence was broken.

Parker spoke, "Y'all ain't going back there. Not unless y'all want to. Do one of y'all want to?"

I stared at him wondering if this was a trick question. What kind of question was that? Why did we leave in the first place was my real concern. What was Parker doing? One of the girls spoke for me, saying "what's going on?"

Parker answered, "Those dudes are shaky. I don't like how they are doing business. Y'all girls are the only ones I felt I could give a chance to. Who's willing to take it?" he asked.

His face was a mixture of seriousness and sincerity. I took a deep breath masked by a half-smile then I asked "Are you serious?.... Are you letting us go?"

One of the other girls interrupted me in a aggravated tone saying, "Letting us go, go where? We ain't got nothing. I ain't got nobody! Y'all tripping."

Parker spoke out in a more aggressive tone, "Look, I ain't in the business of playing hero. I know my business ain't right but whatever. I'm just trying give y'all a break. If you wanna go back I'll take you. I'm out regardless."

"Let her speak for herself. I ain't seen my family in a whole year. I have a mother who probably thinks I am dead. Please send me home."

Parker asked where was home for her and she told him Virginia. "If I let you call somebody am I gonna have to look over my back for cops?" Parker said.

"No, no," she pleaded. "I won't mention you or anybody. I'm just trying to get to my family."

Looking at this girl closely I began to see the innocence behind her make-up. I could tell she was young, maybe fifteen years old. I imagined she was probably taken walking from school. I wasn't much older but I felt a little more hip to life than she was.

Parker looked at me. "What about you? Where's home?"

I responded, "I don't know anymore. All I have is a little brother out there."

"Where is out there?"

"New York."

"New York," he mimicked me. "I knew you were from New York. You always had that thing about you."

"What thing?"

"That…Never mind." he paused and directed his attention to the menu.

The waitress came over. "Ready over here?"

"Yeah, give us four lunch specials with orange juice," Parker ordered. I knew he was just ordering to be cordial, because I knew that none of our minds were on eating anymore. Parker explained the plan would be to drop homegirl back to her hell motel, put the tainted young virgin on a bus home. Then he asked what I wanted to do. "You want a bus too?"he asked. I asked if I could get just a little more time to think.

"Think quick," he said as he asked the waitress to pack our food to-go. Our first stop was as he stated. We dropped the first girl at the gate of the motel. It made no sense watching her walk back willingly to that place but it was her decision. Little Virginia made a call from the phone booth just down the road. This was, of course, a cinematic scene to watch as she sobbed uncontrollably.

Hearing the voice of whoever that was on the other line. I knew that if she could she would teleport through those phone lines and back into her mother's arms. I looked over to notice Parker with a slight glisten in his eyes, as he had to know that what he was doing was the right thing. She thanked Parker continuously, straight up until the time the bus was loading for departure. But I also could read in Parker's eyes the guilt he felt for being what held this young girl away from her loved ones for so long. Like a concerned older brother, he stayed until he saw the bus pull off. I wondered if his conscience could survive knowing that, although he hadn't snatched her off the street himself, he had profited from her demise.

Now it was obvious that the attention would be on me. "Have you thought about what you're going to do?" I just looked at him.

"May I ask which way you rolling?" he said.

"I can't tell you where I'm gonna end up," I interrupted.

"What?" he asked.

My comfort dropped until he suddenly let out a chuckle. "Look, if you do decide to head back to the Big Apple, you can ride with me a little closer in that direction. I'm heading east anyways. Fair?" he asked.

"Fair," I answered.

We began to drive as the R&B tunes played on the radio. Every now again we would catch ourselves singing out the same part, yet acting as if we didn't notice one another's voice. It was apparent after awhile why Parker didn't fit into the cliché of a pimp. He was too laid back. If his job was to be a pimp, and I was his boss, I'd have to say even I would fire him. He wasn't cut for it. He had a heart. Not to dismiss the fact that he was truly still a criminal. It's just that, this specific crime was out of his character.

I sensed Parker didn't feel comfortable speaking too much to me, and I could understand why. Besides, I didn't want him to tell me anything that would put me in danger. I played my position until an old school song came on the radio. Al Green's "Let's Stay Together". My excitement put my voice in full range.

"What you know about this little girl?"

"Little girl, shucks you ain't that old."

"Older than you I know. Matter of fact how old are you?"

"Grown."

"How grown?" he answered.

"Guess," I said.

"Don't make me do that, tell me."

"Eighteen."

"Eighteen, ha. I thought you were in your 20's how you spoke about being grown, so confident?"

"Well ole G., how old are you?"

"Nunyah"

"What kind of language is that?"

"Nunyah business," he answered with a joyful laugh. I had no choice but laugh at myself for falling into that trap.

At this time I guess you can say the laughter broke the ice, 'cause now we were more riding together. Less like ex-captive and kidnapper but more like acquaintances resembling friends. Parker was very handsome. Especially when he smiled. It had been a while since I really noticed how a man looked. I had made a habit of blurring out the faces of all the men I encountered. I hoped that I couldn't really see them, because I knew in truth that even though they had seen my nakedness, none of them never really saw "me". The only image I allowed myself to see were the memories in the back of mind about Lovelle. Sometimes I could find myself in a daze thinking about him. Speaking of a daze, Parker just interrupted the current one I was having.

"Treasure, I got to stop driving for a bit. Unless you can drive we gone have to pull off to one of these truck stops or motels."

I looked at him, "No motels!"

He saw the alarm in my face and I believe he knew instantly and instinctively why I went into a panic.

"I get you. What if it's a decent hotel just for the night? A little HBO, something to eat, then back on the road tomorrow?"

I looked at him with the surprise that my opinion actually mattered. I kept wondering when he would flip from being so nice, to realizing that he still had total control over me.

"Don't worry, I got you!" he said.

My mind paused as I wrapped my mind around this statement for a minute. I reflected back to the last time I had heard these words. They were from Nana. One night when I was quite young I woke up screaming from a bad dream. My Nana ran to my bedside as tears of fright poured from my eyelids. She asked me "what happened?"

As we turned and walked toward the elevator he commented on how well I looked without all of the makeup. I couldn't help but blush and he couldn't either.

"Matter of fact, the room is 609. Go to the room without me. I have to handle something first." He passed me the key, I took the elevator to the 6th floor and I walked into our room for the evening.

"Wow." was my response as I look around at how clean and beautiful things were. I hadn't seen a decent hotel room since Disney World, Florida. With this moment of privacy I chose to go back into my childish ways. I flopped onto the bed, grabbed a pillow and began to roll back and forward on the bed. I grabbed the remote control. "Television" I said to myself. How long has it been since I had watched one of these?

I sat enthused for a minute, watching what my Nana used to call "the picture show" on the screen. I just sat flickering channels. Surprised about all that I had been missing. Eventually two hours had passed without a sight of Parker. I wondered what was up with him. But after a second thought, I wondered if I should I care.

Maybe he had left me here. Maybe we were followed by the cops or even the old partners were looking for us. I worried myself into a temporary panic. Wondering should I leave before someone was after me. "Calm down Cindy," I said to myself. "Breathe." I sat back on the bed and opened the complimentary water that sat on the table. Suddenly there was a knock on the door.

"Oh no, who's that?" said my anxious inner thought. I hope it wasn't the hotel telling me I'm out of here. I walked slowly toward the door while asking, "Who is it?"

"Me."

"Who?"

"Its Parker. Open the door."

I grasped for my first real breath since my mini panic attack. It was really Parker so I opened. "Help me with these few bags." He said.

"What's this?" I asked.

"You left all your stuff so I had to find a mall to pick some things up for both of us. Especially for you. You need better clothes. I hope you can fit a size 7 shoe, that's all I saw."

I didn't know what to say, I just grabbed the things as he passed them to me. I didn't know what to think of this random kindness. But after a while I figured it out. Me looking like I had just come off the corner would only draw attention. And that was exactly what we didn't need. Still, Parker had great taste. I couldn't believe what I was pulling out of the bags were actually mine. I mean, a day ago I was working for him and his partners getting no money, and now I was getting treated to this fanciness.

This was too confusing and tricky. Why was he doing all this? You know it's really something when kindness raises suspicion. I had been so far removed from feeling that I was worth anything, that I naturally began to reject kindness. Something bad was always coming down the pipeline. I just waited to see what it was this time.

Parker sat at the head of the bed, plotted a pillow behind his neck and turned the channel on the television. It surprised me that he flicked right past all the X-rated and R-rated movies and went straight to a comedy. Never really took him for a guy with a sense of humor, but hey. What did I know?

I removed myself from the room, offering him his private time as I went into the bathroom and locked the door. I modeled my new outfits in the mirror and imagined the adoration from people when I walked by. I tucked all of the tags in my pockets like I would usually do after Big Richie would take me shopping. Some people used to laugh at that, but I didn't mind. I kept them in there until at least the first wash. I would take a peep at them when I got dressed to remind myself of how stunning I needed to feel. After my little while of playing dress up I put all my new things back into the bag. I used the rest of the time to get together my personal thoughts. Here I was in a hotel, a mark up from a motel but still here with a man. I didn't know how comfortable to feel. Surely, he was not a John. But I wondered if after this gesture of kindness, would he require something from me. And if so, what would it be? After came a crazy thought. If Parker didn't want sex from me, how would I feel about that?

I had been so conditioned to being treated like a piece of meat, I really forgot if there was any other type of interaction I could have with a man.

"Cindy, get it together." I said under my breath. Parker's voice interrupted

"You alright in there? Hope there is air freshener."

I opened the door with a half smirk on my face. "I wasn't using the bathroom, funny guy."

He said, "Well good, sit with me and watch this new show. It's crazy!"

We both sat on the bed. I sat initially in the far corner until eventually I found myself lying across the bed as we laughed ourselves to tears.

I hadn't heard myself laugh in such a long time. I felt pounds lighter as I giggled some of my worries away. As late night approached, my eyelids began to tire. I was curious to how this sleeping arrangement would play out. Would he gather a sheet and pillow and get on the floor? Would I have to grab the floor or would we lay together? To tell the truth, as nervous as I wanted to be something kept telling me not to worry. Things would all play out fine.

"Cindy, I'm tired and we gotta get up early so take the bed."

He stood from the bed and walked himself into the bathroom. I didn't waste any time. I nestled myself deeply under the sheets in a fetal position. It's funny, but I don't recall seeing Parker even exit the bathroom. I was just that tired. Sleep fell upon me like I had stayed awake for a whole year.

I recall my dream that night very vividly. I remembered standing in front of my old apartment. The one in which I lived with my Nana. I kept knocking and knocking. No answer. I then decided to slide a note under the door. The letter said, "It's Cindy, I came to see you. I'll come back Nana." A second after I slid the note under the door, the door opened. I turned back to see a little girl looking about five years old holding the letter. It was so strange that the little girl never moved her mouth and neither did I, but it's like I heard her saying "Take this letter."

I told her without words to keep it. It was for Nana. I asked her to tell my Nana that I had come by to see her. The little girl then released the letter from her hand but instead of dropping quickly to the floor the letter seemed like it slowly floated back into my hands. I kept my eyes on this letter as it placed itself back between my fingers. And by the time it was gripped into my hands, I looked over and both the door and the little girl were gone. I looked to what became only a brick wall, knelt to my knees and began to cry uncontrollably. But in between my sobs I looked down at the letter and it was Nana's writing. "Home is never far. When you find it, you'll find me."

What was this riddle? What did it mean? These questions remained in my thoughts until the moment I opened my eyes. I didn't know if I could ever understand what home was again.

A little in a haze but without hesitation I dressed myself in a cool get-together, grabbed my things, and followed Parker out of the hotel and into the car. I sat in the passenger seat, looking out of the window as Parker stuck the key in the ignition. Call it coincidence but when he turned on the radio, what was playing?

None other than "Home" by Stephanie Mills. Before she gotten to the first words "I wish I was home" my eyes began to cloud. Parker looked toward me almost as if to ask what was wrong, but he said nothing. He gave me a brush and a pat on my knee as he continued to pull off. Five songs into the ride, my thoughts began to clear. The sign on the highway said Route 95 heading east. Parker seemed to be in his own zone as he dipped and dodged through traffic. The way he was driving, I didn't want to disturb him because although I was not quite clear on where I was heading, I did know I wanted to arrive there alive.

I drifted off into a cat nap. When I woke up signs read Virginia: 2 miles. Parker parked his car on the side of this gas station, jumped out and walked over to the closest pay phone. I observed this was no ordinary call. First, I watched Parker look suspiciously around, appearing to be on a lookout for something. Between moments his voice would raise and hands would swing into the air. After he must have put a dozen coins into the phone, Parker turned and walk towards the car. When he got in and sat down, I looked over to him and extended my hand as to return his friendly patting favor, but he shoved my hand quickly away.

"Don't be hitting me," I spoke abruptly.

He yelled back "Shut the hell up! I ain't hit you. Just don't touch me!"

"I just was…"

"You were nothing. Just don't say anything."

I could hear the seriousness in his tone. I snapped my teeth and turned my face to look out the side view mirror. Seconds after, Parker sighed loud and long. He reclined his seat and folded his hands behind his head, staring at the ceiling of the car as if he were watching a comet falling from a red sky. His was looking so hard it seemed he could see straight through the car. Since my mood was already disrupted, I chose not to question what was on his mind. I really didn't need a confrontation with him. At this point I realized he was all I had, therefore, I was at his mercy.

Two miles of silence and we were in Virginia. Parker finally spoke again.

"Never mind a couple of minutes ago, just had to get myself together. No offense to you, alright Cindy?"

I just looked at him. I nodded my head in agreement, understanding that sometimes emotions could get the best of us.

Parker then asked the question. "Are you sure about New York? Because this here is the furthest we are traveling together."

One part of me wanted to ask if I could continue on with him, but the other didn't want to be reminded of the immediate past I was trying to run away from.

"It's cool, Parker," I responded. "You could put me on any bus from this point."

Parker stared at me as he noticed the defeat of my posture.

"Cindy, I can tell you're not anxious to leave. I'm good on picking up on things and I know you are scared. But look at it this way. At least you have a choice to what you want your life to be. You definitely didn't have that two days ago."

He briefly started to explain he was at a similar point in his journey. But he cut himself short and just said, "Just hold on, Youngin."

"Youngin?" I interrupted.

"Yes, Youngin. Look at it this way. You're stepping back in town looking pretty fresh. If you don't paint your story on you face, who will ever know?"

My curiosity became overwhelming at that moment. I just had to ask him the question. So I did.

"Parker," I said in a small voice.

"Yea, what up?"

"You are so different. How did you ever find yourself in this line of work?"

"Tangled webs," he said. "Just make sure you never find yourself in one. They are hard to get out of once your in."

With that answer, I knew it was time for me to go. With nothing more to do but thank him, we pulled up to a Greyhound station. He passed me a small grip of cash in my hand, patted me on the shoulder, and watched me walk up the steps unto the bus. I found a seat near the window and I watched Parker drive away.

With fifteen minutes before departure, I people watched as I awaited the unknown. I watched mothers with their children, young couples, elder folks, working people, all riding on the same bus as me. I wondered what awaited them all in the city. Would there be someone waiting for them when they arrived? I knew for certain no one would be there for me.

This knowledge hurt like hell. I just need God to lead me, because everything I had was in this bag. And this bag could never be home.

I sat through the uncomfortableness of my ride, thinking of all or nothing I would return to. I left a school girl I returned a woman. I thought of Little Richie Boo and my mother. But what most I thought about was vengeance. I hated Big Richie with a cruel passion. I imagined appearing before him like a ghost. Surely he had wanted me dead because he sent me into the arms of danger. God help me, but I saw his life with as little value as he has seen mine.

I feared him not! I cared the least about how powerful he may have been or what else he could have done to me. My soul had already been destroyed by the animals he sent me to. My thoughts were dangerous. My mind weary until eventually I put myself back to sleep.

Anxiety was beginning to destroy me, so I needed every bit of rest before I was back in the city. I woke only a stop away from Grand Central, Port Authority. My eyes melted into the highway, the same way they had the first night I was transported. The only difference was, there was nothing obstructing my view. I counted the signs. Every mile, every half mile until we approached the city.

Now seeing the traffic of Manhattan I knew the time had finally arrived.

We turned into the garage of the station. People stood as the bus slowed to a stop, anxious to deploy. And I didn't share the same feeling. The fact was, I had more roads to go. And I wasn't sure where they would lead. All the telephone numbers I had known were erased from my mind. And I didn't know where to begin on this journey. The city looked all new and very intimidating. But despite what I felt, I knew I had to move forward. So that's what I did.

NEW YORK PITY

It wasn't long before I was introduced to the New York state of mind. The pushing and shoving; the hustle and bustle. I managed most of the way to the token clerk and asked for directions back into Brooklyn. I never really became accustomed to the trains before. Guess I never had anywhere to go outside of my area. Still, I did my best not to seem startled by the congestion of the platform. I hopped on the first hot rails toward Brooklyn. Every new stop appeared like a movie. The characters that came on and off the train were hilarious. The fashion had taken a definite twist. And the conversations were entertaining.

People seemed to watch me just as close. I wondered what they were thinking as they looked at me. I don't imagine I looked like the hell I just came out of. In fact, I was a well dressed mess. You see, looks can be deceiving. Everything that I owned was in this traveling bag, little did they know.

Finally my train stop approached. As soon as the doors opened I felt my heart skip a beat. I walked outside the turnstile and up the stairs. The first sight of familiar territory for me almost made my eyes well up with tears. One part of me wanted to run and jump, the other wanted to sit on the sidewalk and cry out all my pains. A million thoughts and emotions raced through my head. I must have missed two lights before I crossed the street. The moon, the noise, the crowds around the corner bodegas all made me wonder how much had I really missed.

Same ole men in front of the liquor store. Young guys still blocked the doorway of the chicken spot. The curses and swears still resound from the Chinese restaurant. Although dysfunctional, It was comforting. It made me feel like I hadn't missed out on too much.

I walked a couple of blocks to where the environment seemed to lighten up. Now where do I go? Cindy, I thought to myself, find somebody.

Who could I pop up on? Who would accept me in? What if everybody had moved? It suddenly fell on me like a ton of bricks. I'm homeless. Even after all I've been through, I felt just as vulnerable as in those dingy motels.

I remember at the beginning of my whole ordeal I had a thousand escape plans. Where I would run, who I would tell, what they would do. But once time got a hold of me it all began to fade. I was trapped in my negative thoughts for a while. I knew I couldn't survive day to day imagining love awaited me. Hope would of just made me weak. I needed my strength. Friends and family had just become faces with no stories in my dreams. I hardly heard their voices. It all just faded with time.

Just when a new set of depression was beginning, something happened that took me straight out of my daze. I was standing before another street corner and I heard, "Excuse me sweet, Do you have a light?"

I didn't even feel anybody walk up on me, but then again I wasn't paying attention. I lifted my head and turned to say "no" but before I could, the person yelled "Oh damn, aren't you?"

I then began to focus in on this guy and realized I knew him. It was Shantell's cousin. This was one of those moments where you would hear my Nana say "Now look how God works."

Although I never paid him much attention before, all of a sudden his name popped up in my head. "Rudy," I said.

"Yeah Ma. You're my cousin's peoples, right? She was just talking about you the other day. She said she ain't know what happened to you."

"Yeah well, Rudy, do you know where she is now?"

"Yeah she lives with me now. Come on, I'll take you to her. First let me grab a lighter from that store."

This was perfect, I thought. Shantell is the right person to see right now. Besides, I've missed her. I knew she would not have one problem helping me figure things out. And that's exactly what I needed to do: figure things out.

As I walked with Rudy, we made small talk asking each other minor questions and giving even shorter answers. Before long we were in front of his house, and just in the nick of time. As we're coming up the stairs, Shantell and a guy were coming out the door. First it seemed they would just walk past us until Rudy yanked her arm back and said "What you don't speak to my company?"

Shantell took a closer look into my face followed shortly with a scream. I think she screamed herself into a shock because her eyes looked like she had just seen a ghost. This to me felt so good. She embraced me. Looked at me again, then embraced me a second time.

"Girl, where? What? Why?" She mixed into a jumble. "Never mind, wait, I be with you. Rudy, take her in!"

Besides my own excitement, I had to chuckle at the fact that Shantell didn't change. She still wouldn't ever let you get a word in once she got going. Well, I walked in, sat on the couch and waited. She must have just walked her company downstairs because she was back only a few moments after.

"C, what happened to you? You were on some unsolved mystery sh##!"

"Yo, I can't tell you everything but all I could say it was Big Richie's fault. He set me up."

My voice then began to grumble.

"What you mean, C? I went by your house the day after. I saw your door was held open by some boxes. It was apparent there was some moving going on. Big Richie came to the door and said y'all were moving. I was like 'What happened? Cindy didn't say goodbye.' When I asked where you were he said you were at the new place getting things set up. To tell the truth, I was pissed. I was like why wouldn't you tell me, of all people, you were going. But after a while it seemed kind of not like you. I knew at some point you would have called me or stopped by."

"Shantell, I couldn't. I didn't even know I was gonna be gone. Remember we were supposed to meet up with Lovelle and them? I mean, if I told you what I went through all this time you wouldn't believe me. Big Richie tried to have me killed."

"C, are you serious? I'm saying you're alive so you couldn't call somebody, even the police? Remember what happened to Tanya."

"I know" I sighed.

"Speaking of Tanya, I saw your cousin Dessa about last year. She asked me about you. She said she hasn't heard from you either. She was real worried. So worried that if I would have listened to her and the dream she said she had, we would have been searching in the morgue.

But you know me, I just was think it as her being paranoid especially from Tanya's death."

"Do you have her number?" I asked.

"No, but I know she said she was back in New York. Atlanta wasn't for her. C, you should look her up, she looked like she was doing OK."

"Yeah, well I know but first things first. I have to find my mother and brother. Ever heard about them?"

"You know, I thought I saw your mother a few times. This

woman looked like her. But I thought, naw, because this woman acted like she was smoking or something. I never bothered to speak. We know how fly your mom stay."

"For real? She looked like her? Where?" I asked anxiously,

I had a hunch that the person Shantell saw could have been my mom and if I found her Little Richie couldn't be far.

"Somewhere in the Crown Heights section. But it has been a while C, don't get your hopes up" Shantell said with a sad expression.

"I know, I just gotta think, you know?"

"I hear you."

Rudy sat on the couch listening to our conversation looking so shocked and concerned. I know sometimes a situation like this can make people speechless. But the words he found to say was all I needed to hear at that moment.

"Well C, if you ain't got nowhere to be, stay with us. It's not a problem, you always seemed cool."

"I appreciate and I might have to do that." I answered.

The rest of night played out mid tempo. I wound up telling Shantell so many stories that she began to get as upset and vengeful as I was. Big Richie was a target. She spoke about sending guys for him and a bunch of stuff. Lucky for us sleep fell upon us with the sun rise, because we became so worked up that we weren't even rational anymore.

We thought we were in a gangsta movie. Shantell still was my ride or die. We woke up in the late afternoon. Both of us had a pounding headache and desperately needed something to eat. Shantell's cousin must have known how we felt because before we could wash our faces he was walking in the door with breakfast.

"C, do you eat bacon?" Rudy asked.

"Yeah, thanks a lot," I answered.

While walking in the bathroom, I closed the door ran the water and looked in the mirror. "Cindy, Cindy, Cindy" I said to myself. "What are you going to do?" I stared at the dried up tears on my face and told myself as I always did "get it together."

I wiped off my face and walked back into the living room where Shantell and Rudy sat eating bacon, egg and cheese sandwiches. "Yours is right there C," she pointed. "Eat, because we got some figuring out to do."

You know when you've been through so much on your own, it feels good to have someone take your burdens as theirs. I wanted to smile but my face wouldn't let me so I sat, ate and tuned out to the noise of the television.

"C, when my friend comes by with the car I'm going to ask him to drop us over there where I think I saw your mom last. Maybe we'll get lucky, you know?"

"Yeah that sounds great."

"Y'all got money?" Rudy asked.

Shantell answered, "You know me Cuz," with a boastful attitude. "And C's with me so it don't matter." I looked at Shantell as I wondered how could she be so arrogant about money. She made it sound as though it comes easy to her. If so, I needed to know how she's getting it.

Four years is a long time but not that long.

When the time turned to 4 o'clock we were dressed and ready to leave. Shantell commented on my clothes and how fresh they were.

"Damn C, I almost felt sorry for you but you flyer than me," she laughed.

"Haha," I smirked as I knew that I did look kinda decent for someone who just came from what I've come from, but she did have to tell me lighten up on the make-up. I knew I looked border line drag queen. Guess it was just one of those things I picked up along the way to hide myself. I knew I had to let it go.

Soon after we heard a car beep. Shantell grabbed the keys saying, "C, lets go." I followed straight after her down the stairs and once we opened the front door I looked at bright expensive truck that awaited us. My mind said "hold up" because as we got closer to the ride I could see that the guy driving the truck was so flashy that his diamonds could have blinded me. He looked somewhere between the ages of 35 and 90, that is he definitely wasn't in our age brackets. I opened the back door to the car and sat. Shantell jumped in the front seat, leaned over and gave this man a kiss. One thing was for certain: this wasn't the guy from last night.

He looked back over the front seat and said "Who's this?"

"This is my girl C I grew up with."

"I ain't ever heard of C before."

"And you ain't ever heard of breath mint before either, turn around and drive."

I wanted to laugh simply because Shantell has always been quick at the lips and sassy. I just was so surprised this man who could be old enough to be her father just stood her taking control like that. Life can be funny and unpredictable. Shantell played passenger driver and before we know it we were pulling over on this side street.

"C, wait outside for me" Shantell asked.

I stood a little bit off to the back of the car but close enough that I could hear and see them. I watched him reach behind his seat and pull up a small leather bag. He passed Shantell something out of it.

Shortly after, Shantell jumped out the car walked up to me and said, "Now let's get a cab."

"Hold up," I interrupted.

"Why didn't we just let him drops us where we needed to be?"

"C, you can't let these men know ya moves, that's just my money man. I'm not rockin any ole G in broad daylight." She laughed sarcastically.

"Money man....okay"

"Yeah real money C, and as a matter fact. Take this."

She passed me five hundred dollar bills. "Since you're my homegirls, if I'm right you gotta be right."

It was obvious that Shantell has been dealing major since I've been gone. I would have asked her how she was getting money but it seemed a little too obvious. I mean who carries money like that outside? It sort of reminded me of Big Richie and how my mom were. After our little chat, our next ride arrived we jumped in a taxi cab. "Get me to Fulton Street." Shantell told the driver. We were headed on our way and I began to try and ease my anxiety. Was it really a possibility that I was going to see my mother and brother soon? As we drove along we passed by people on the streets knowing my family could possibly be anyone of them.

Who knew that I would actually ever be curious to see my mother? I think I stopped waiting for her when I was about five years old and even then it wasn't critical. I could hardly hear Shantell talking to me during the ride. I was too distracted in my daydreams to really participate in any conversation.

Well, a few minutes later we arrived at the destination. The cab driver said the fare was ten dollars. From the response Shantell gave him you would have thought he said a million dollars. She literally cussed him down to an even $7. I believe that if she had two more minutes with him she would have made him pay for us to get out of his car. It was funny and ridiculous at the same time that Shantell and I had pockets full of money, but still she was so cheap. Shantell had this new bossy thing about her but I thought: if it works her, hey!

"I saw her around this area, let's get to asking some questions," Shantell said.

We walked and walked. We stopped anybody who seemed native to the neighborhood, until we eventually walked our way into a little eatery. Shantell and I were both hungry and tired and we should have worn comfortable shoes. Looking like models was not helping us to much, in fact we looked foolish.

As we sat, we found humor in all the interesting people who walked in and by the window. It's funny how you can always find people airing all of their dirty laundry in public. And since we were still young and immature in lots of ways, we laughed openly, happy to take advantage of a little time spent not worrying.

"C, what are you going to do?"

"What you mean Shantell?" I asked.

"I mean there are thousands of people out here. Finding your mother will be like finding a needle in a haystack. You don't have anybody to call and ask about her?"

I shook my head, partly in disgust, and partly in sadness because I truly knew no one I could call.

Shantell sipped the last of her juice and said, "C'mon, this is dumb! We'll find them a smarter way!" I let Shantell take the lead because I had run out of ideas, and the rain looked like it was coming.

We flagged another cab and went back to her apartment. We threw ourselves onto the couches and everything was quiet for a moment. I interrupted the silence with a question. "Shantell, what's going on out here? What I gotta do to survive out here?"

She gave me a look and said "It depends on you C. How you wanna do things?"

Without giving me a chance to respond, she continued, "People struggling, especially at our age. Girls got babies doing the welfare way while others are flipping burgers. But then, some get it like me."

"Like you?" I mirrored her with my body gesture and all. "How exactly are you getting it?" I asked.

"C, I know you've been through a lot but what I'm doing isn't a cake walk. I take chances."

"Yeah well I see those chances keep your pockets alright!"

"Oh yeah, some money stay in my pockets but I do roll with some dangerous cats."

"Who? like that guy that picked us up?" I asked.

"No C. that's just one of my side hustles."

"OH, side hustles, excuse me," I chuckled with sarcasm.

"Cindy for real this is big woman stuff. This isn't a joke." I saw the seriousness in her face, and I silenced my laughter. "If you really want to know, I run product," she said.

"Sell drugs, Shantell?" I asked hastily.

"Chill C. You act like you don't know anything about that."

It wasn't like I didn't know; it's just that I was surprised that she did. I listened as Shantell broke down the operation. She explained how her cousin Rudy operated , and how staying well-kept fit into the whole scheme of things. I admit the whole thing was pretty compelling. I mean, I didn't have anything but a ninth grade education and I needed money. We spoke for a little while longer, but it didn't take much to convince me that I wanted in. Lord knows it had some downfalls, but desperation is a compromising state of mind.

The next day Shantell prepped me for the introduction to the man who made everything happen for her. She paid extra attention to how I looked. Even giving me some of her clothes to hook up with what I had.

"OK C, this is the deal. You gotta be fly! He ain't gonna mess with no dusty looking chicks. Also, only answer the questions that he asks. Don't do any extra talking or nothing. He can't stand a person who has a big mouth. He says people who talk too much are a poison to the operation."

I listened closely to Shantell although I thought it sounded really ironic coming from the biggest mouth person I knew.

"And yeah, don't look all nervous, like you not hip to the game, because if you can't handle the role, you won't get to play it." I nodded in agreement, and then we got ready to leave. As we walked out of the door, I heard a voice in my head saying Cindy this ain't for you. But of course I shook it off. I figured that voice wasn't putting a roof over my head so I had to do what I had to do.

Eventually we met up with the guy. I presumed he would have this big drug dealer intimidating look but instead he looked more like a janitor. He looked no older than his late twenties, clean shaven and a little chubby. He showed no signs of having any real money. In fact besides the one diamond pinky ring he really had nothing flashy about him. It was confusing to think that this was the guy that Shantell raved about. But putting the stereotype aside, by the end of this meeting this guy was telling me he would be like a big brother to me. He told me to watch and play things the same way that I had watched Shantell and I would be fine. If I didn't know better you would think I was being welcomed into some kind of wholesome family or something.

Shantell glowed with excitement of having her sidekick at her side. A small part of me appreciated just being accepted. Although this might mean consequences I wasn't ready to deal with, I welcomed the feeling of belonging it gave me to work with Shantell.

I adjusted quickly to this lifestyle. Shantell and I partied uncontrollably. Alcohol was our new best friend, which seemed like the lesser evil. I finally felt that I was controlling my own destiny. After a few months, looking for Denise and my brother faded to the back of my mind. I was having too much fun! Shantell and I shopped almost every day, blew money on restaurants, hung out with rich men and in places where we weren't even old enough to be. Life was good.

We had the interest of every guy who was curious to know how we were rolling. Before I knew it, I felt like I was full fledged involved in everything that was going on in my city. I was building relationships between people who kept my money flowing in, so how could I complain.

By the time my twenty-first birthday rushed around, I was driving an expensive car, wearing diamonds, enjoying my popularity, and had attitude that wouldn't wait.

Shantell and I were living rather well until she caught the love bug, right when we were at the top of our game. Right at our apex, Shantell decided to go and get pregnant. This, of course, changed everything about the way we had to move. The apartment that we shared was no longer big enough to bring a little one into, so eventually she moved in with the baby's father. Not a good look at all! Her baby's father was very possessive. He started to monitor where she went and who she kept ties to until eventually Shantell and I began to stray from each other.

Still, I was very happy for her when the baby came. I was able to buy the baby everything he could have possibly needed. And despite the child's father disapproval (I didn't care for him anyways, so the feeling was mutual) Shantell named me the Godmother. I really hoped Shantell was just going through a phase with this guy, but by the time the baby turned one, Shantell and I were only speaking once in a while. I wished her the best, but it did hurt. It changed everything about the way I moved. I didn't have those extra set of eyes around. Besides that, Shantell had always been the one to come up with new ideas and schemes that most times worked. Now it was all on me.

My circle changed and eventually I became my own best friend. I didn't have too much of a conscience about anything I did anymore. I went from not wanting a man to breathe on me to not being able to live without the attention I could only get from a man.

I was used to people putting me in the spotlight by now, but nothing compared to the night of my twenty-fifth birthday. At this period of time, I was surrounded by all of the Who's Who of the city. The money I made came with influence. Influence, of course, gave me a little power. People just wanted to be around me to learn or feel protected. But the kind of attention I got on this birthday was even more unique. Associates of mine gave me a party at a bar. The theme was masquerade, so it was hard to make out who was there at first. Usually I was too paranoid to be in any surroundings without knowing all of what was going on around me, but for this I made an exception.

There were all types of celebrities in the house, catering to my every need, so I was surprised when someone walked over to my table and said, "Some gentleman over there would like you to come and have a toast with him."

As my eyes tried to see in the direction he pointed to, I wound up just sending him back with the message, "It's my day, whoever wants me needs to come to me!"

Between the champagne and my newly founded sassiness, I knew I came off arrogant but I didn't care. I was just absorbed in my own hype and the energy of the club. Just a few moments later a body stood right in the middle of my sight. And WHOA, was it a sight! There before me was a tall sexy man, who leaned over to speak into my ear. With my mind still a bit distracted and with the dimness of the club I couldn't make out this man's face. Eventually I heard this voice say "Long time no see." I suddenly sobered up enough to realize that I knew him. I looked closer at the smile and realized it was Lovelle.

"Oh my goodness!" I yelled.

Through the loud music I asked what he was doing here. Lovelle told me that he ran into Loud Mouth and she told him where to find me. I laughed as I remembered that that was what he used to call Shantell.

"Wow Cindy, You look good! Happy Birthday."

'Thanks," I answered. "You looking fine yourself."

Lovelle smirked in that way that made me remember when in high school. In fact, it turned me on the same way it did then. He grabbed my hand and pulled me toward him and before I knew it we were downstairs of the club in a better lit lounge area. I can't explain the surprise I felt being next to him.

I'd been dreaming about this guy since I could remember and the last thing I heard about him was that he had gone away to college. Now, here he was. Lovelle was manlier now, still handsome and as real and sincere as I always remembered. After a little talking, we exchanged numbers and he left the party. I eventually continued to dance my night away, but I couldn't wait to call him. I just couldn't wait.

I don't remember how I got home that night but I could remember his face in between my hangover and makeup-covered pillow. I knew I had experienced a long night, but that was to be expected. I finally lifted my body from the bed and went into the bathroom. I washed my face and ran a shower. I found myself overcome with childlike giggles and blushes. I made imaginary conversations with Lovelle and wished that he was right there with me. I fantasized about him turning the knob of the door and joining me but all I had was the warmth of the thought because I knew it wouldn't happen.

I jumped out the shower, put on my sweetest scent and threw on my kick-around sweats. I was still not fully refreshed; I still felt drained from the night before, but I was equally as anxious to call the number Lovelle gave me. Although I was excited to talk to him, I didn't want to seem desperate. Besides, if he had asked anybody about me recently, he would know I had it going on.

I figured I would eat a bite and lounge for a while since it was still early, but before I knew it was noon. My phone began to ring.

"C, what's up?" the voice spoke.

At first with all the background noise I couldn't make out the person clearly, but then I realized it was Shantell.

"What's going on girl?" I asked.

"Was my present the biggest one you got?"

I paused for a second and then laughed.

"What, Lovelle?"

"Hell yeah Lovelle! Don't act like you ain't hyped, matter fact tell him to wake up!" she said laughing.

"Naw, Shantell, he's not here," I giggled.

"Oh really, what happened? You know he's the love of your life."

Shantell went on and on until my mind was eventually distracted by the knock on the door. I looked through the peephole and in disbelief I opened the door.

"Girl, I'm gonna call you back." I didn't even hear her response before I hung up.

"Lovelle, What are you doing here? How did you know where I lived?"

"You're hilarious,"he said. "How do you think you got home?

With a bewildered look , I said, "You mean…"

"Yes," he interrupted.

"Wow I must have been…"

"Really drunk?"Lovelle interrupted again.

We both laughed. But oh, was I really embarrassed. He came in and sat in my living room.

"Cindy, when I came back to the club you was there but you were out of it. Your friend told me where you lived, and I drove you here. You seemed OK enough to open your door and go in, so I went home when you got inside."

My eyes widened as I was still total disbelief that I could not remember any of this happening. I kept thinking Cindy that was so stupid! What is wrong with you?! I imagined what I looked like in front of him being as drunk as I was. But while I was beating myself up he asked, "What's our plans for today?"

"Excuse me, OUR?" I asked.

"Yeah OUR," he responded.

"How you know I haven't got plans of my own. I am a busy woman!" I said this was as much sassiness I could get away with and still seem sexy.

"So what, I'm not worth a change of plans?" He answered back in a similar manner, matching me stride for stride. .

Then we paused and looked each other in the eyes. Both of

us with a half-smile and goo-goo eyes. "Well I guess I can work something out. Doesn't seem that I have a choice, do I?"

He answered "Nope. You don't!" and laughed.

That day turned into weeks and those weeks into months, and a lot of life in-between. Lovelle and I hit it off really well. He was far beyond the men I kept company with. He had style, good vibes and the level-headedness that was void in my life. I kept plenty of the things I did away from him in fear that he might judge me. It was clear that he taken the intellectual and spiritual path, which made him more grounded than most. I knew what I did in my world would conflict with who he was and whom I wanted him to be in my life.

He tried not to ask me so many personal questions, therefore I didn't volunteer much either. But after a while, so much was going on in my business world that our relationship began to be distracting. While I loved the distraction I knew I was suffering because of it.

I always kept money, although with Lovelle I never needed it. He kept up to all the standards that I heard a real man should, and it as well appreciated. But before I knew it, five months had come and gone, and it was nearing the time for him to leave.

Lovelle had spoken about the fact that he would have to go away for business related reasons, but he never said for how long until one night over a candlelit dinner at one of my favorite restaurants he opened the conversation.

"Cindy, what does this mean for us?"

"What do you mean, Lovelle?" I answered with my head hanging low.

"Look at me, C. I am trying to talk to you."

I looked in his eyes as he reached my hand and squeezed them tightly.

"Cindy, I have to leave for a year and they just told me I have to go to Canada..."

That's when it happened. My stomach quaked my palms began to sweat as my heart raced.

"Canada, a year? Damn Lovelle, why so far?"

I tried to keep my eyes wide to avoid shutting them and letting my tears fall.

"C, when I come back everything could be..."

I interrupted, "Be what...Like it is now, Lovelle? A lot can happen in a year. Hell, a whole lot!"

"C, calm down. Why you acting this way?"

By now I had snatched my hands from his, and leaned back with my arms folded.

"Act? No, I'm not acting. In fact, I think you're the one who's been acting. Acting like you gave a damn. Go Lovelle! Just go and have a good time!" By now my voice had begun to vibrate in a low tone.

"Good time... Is that what you think? I'm leaving to better myself and you're acting like a selfish brat. And acting... the only thing I've been acting like is loving you, and I believed it until now. I see what you're about Cindy!" he wiped his mouth with the napkin and pushed his plate aside.

"Love me," I said sarcastically as I reached for my jacket. "That's brand new, is that how it's supposed to go. Is this when I'm supposed to blush and turn rosy red?"

He looked me in the eyes and we sat there in a long, a dead silence. After he shook his head and reached as if he were going in his pockets to get money. And that's when I said the rudest thing that could have come in my head and out of my mouth.

"Keep your pity pennies, this break-up ison me."

I wanted to smack myself as soon as I'd said it. How stupid, stupid, stupid. What did I just say? His face turned from me in a way that made any apology seem too late. He just got up and left. As he stormed out, it seemed like every eye in the restaurant was on me. I stirred around at the inquiring eyes and I sucked my teeth while shrugging my shoulders. I had to pretend it didn't affect me in order not to feel embarrassed.

I had another glass of wine before I finally decided to pay the bill. Luckily the weather was nice outside because my shoes were too tight and my heart was shattered. Taxis passed me by one by one. And between screams and swears I wept from my own behavior. Eventually I reached home, and I just went to my bed and cried. I knew I had messed up. Why did I do that? I just couldn't figure out. He just told me that he loved me for the first time, which I have been waiting to hear from him since I was a teenager and I just totally destroyed the whole moment. Eventually I let the wine put me to sleep, because, although my mind was restless, my heart had enough!

WELL, AFTER I MESSED THAT UP...

Morning eventually came and my first instinct was to check my messages. And to my surprise there were none from Lovelle. This was a sheer indication that last night was not a figment of my imagination. I had really thrown what we had to the dogs and there was no telling if I would ever get it back. My ego told me to take a shower, wash off the memories and resume business as usual, but my heart screamed for me call him as quickly as I could. My faithful defense mechanism let my ego take charge and replenished my old character, the one that didn't care about anything or anyone. I tried to convince myself that he just wanted an excuse to be with someone else, or that his feelings for me weren't sincere but I knew that he really did have feelings for me and this was what hurt me the most.

The rest of my days went by as usual. I was lonely, but with each new morning I found myself accepting that I wasn't meant to be with the love of my life. I made plans, transitioned my mind back to the game and once again made money my lover.

It seemed opportunities had been waiting for me, and I was just playing absentee spending all my time with Lovelle. A few calls, some visits and a couple of hangovers later and I was restored back to my ole self. I began to party like I had lost my mind. I flirted with trouble and lied myself out of love.

Ignorance is comfort to a fool, and I was a fool indeed. I had convince myself it was his loss. And as long as I could act like nothing ever happened, the better I could go on with my life.

Two months passed so quickly. I had bag after bag stacked in my apartment. Everything still had tags on them. Retail therapy I suppose. I even had leftovers piling my refrigerator from lonely dining. All this to convince myself I was happy. I wasn't doing a good job of it because everything began to remind me of Lovelle . One afternoon Shantell called me out of the blue.

"C, get over here, I've got our next move. It's with these out of town cats."

I was very surprised for the call since Shantell hadn't called me much lately, so I responded instantly. When I got to her place, she opened her door decked from head to toe.

"Hold up, Shantell, I thought you traded in your sexiness for a blender. What's up with you?" I said humorously.

"C, stop playing. I met somebody," she remarked back with a smile.

"Well that somebody better have a gun messing around with your crazy baby daddy!"

We both laughed as we both knew that was an understood fact. We sat down at her kitchen table as we began to talk. Shantell began searching through her cabinets for something.

"I know it's here…"

"What's here? And where is my godson?" I asked.

"Your godson is in Virginia with Kimmie and his family. He will be there for like a month."

"What? Kimmie let you out of handcuffs for a month? What did you do Shantell?' I asked.

"Nothing, C. Oh…Here it is."

"Here is what?" I asked.

She pulled out a menu. "What Shantell…a menu? What, so we supposed to stick up a delivery guy?" I said as I laughed.

"No C, I wrote homeboy's number on this when I met him in front of the restaurant. His name is Tyson."

"Who: Mike Tyson? "I said sarcastically.

"No, Tyson Chicken," she said back smiling. "Stop playing, C, this is serious. His name is Tyson and he was posted up in a truck with his boys sweating me real hard the other day. He got out the car and we spoke for a little bit and out of nowhere once he saw how I got down, he started hipping me to some next stuff. You know how I was running my mouth, he knew I wasn't a choir girl. He told me to meet him in Queens today at this address I wrote down." She said all this almost in on breath."Shantell, I am not trying to meet nobody in a dark alley, so what else do you know about him?" I said with a more serious face.

"C'mon C, trust, if I thought he had bad vibes I would have not even told him my style. Remember I was the one that taught you that. This is a barbershop where we will be meeting him and a couple of friends."

"Alright, Shantell, if I sense something strange about them, don't ask me any questions. We are leaving…..deal?" I said.

"Cool I'm with you," she said. "But I'm driving!"

I laughed, remembering how bossy she could be at times.

Eventually we pulled up to the barbershop. It was a nice block and low key, which made me feel a little bit more comfortable. We opened the door and a tall dark-skinned guy with curly hair stood from his chair and went straight toward Shantell.

"Hey cutie," he said while hugging her like he really knew her. "Son, get this beautiful lady and her friend a chair." He ordered two other guys who were sitting around. The two of them stood up like soldiers and offered us their own chairs but I opted to stand instead. "So, Shantell, or shall I say Ms. Brooklyn? I see you're serious about your business, huh?" he said with a flirtatious face.

"I'm here, ain't I?" she answered back with her usual arrogance. "And this is my Girl C, I don't do nothing without her. You see her, you see me."

The guy who hugged Shantell said "Good. 'Cause we about to start this meeting as soon as my cousin comes out the bathroom."

Just as he spoke the words, some guy emerges from a back doorway and simultaneously another older guy comes from out of a door that stood off to the side.

I just stood on the wall taking in my surroundings. I tried not to stare too hard at people, but I did want to make sure I recognized who was around. I let Shantell talk to the guy I now realized was Tyson as the rest of of just stood listening. That is, until I heard him say to Shantell, "This is my cousin Parker," and when I heard him say the name, it's like a light switch came on in my head. I zoomed into this guy's face.

"Parker! O snap" I said to myself. I lifted my purse over my face, which wasn't genius for someone who wanted to hide because it only brought attention toward my way. Parker noticed and ask me to step further out of the corner near the entrance.

"Treasure." Parker called. And my face dropped with embarrassment.

"Yo, give us a few," he said to his cousin as he rushed toward me, grabbed my arm and nearly pushed me out of the door.

"Yo, let go my arm," I said loudly as I understood that all eyes were now on me.

The door of the barbershop closed behind us and we walked toward the side of the building which was out of sight.

"What are you doing here?" he asked.

"What are you doing here?" I asked back.

Parker then removed the shades from off my face and said, "You shouldn't even be around none of this!"

"Around what?" I asked. "I'm with my girl, I don't even know what's going on," I explained. "What's all this about?

"All you need to know is this ain't for no young girls like you," he said like he was my teacher.

"Young girls like me? Hold up… First off, I'm not young. And secondly, you don't even know me to tell me what I should and shouldn't be doing!"

"Oh, I get it. Look at you. All grown and cocky. What… I help you out of the dungeon, now you running into the pit?"

His remark kind of hurt me. Mainly because I had almost forgotten how gracious he was for setting me free. I guess his face reminded me of a dark past that I tried to push to the back of my thoughts. I really reacted toward him like he was the enemy.

"I'm sorry Parker, I'm out of line, you just caught me off guard."

The look in his eyes hinted that he knew that he had probably come off as a little aggressive himself.

Just then Tyson and Shantell came through the door and looked confused and dumbfounded. Parker broke the silence by saying, "Let's get up out of here and go talk."

Shantell looked at me for a sign of approval as I nodded in agreement.

Tyson asked, "So how we riding?"

Shantell answered with "Ya'll could ride with us."

"I don't know, we can't be out on these blocks riding any ole kinda way"

"Oh no, he ain't tryna play us C, what chicks can't ride on fly wheels?

"You really don't know what type of chicks you dealing with, huh?" Shantell said with her usual sassiness. She walked over to the truck and said, "Yes hun, this is us. And I own her twin sister. I have her home parked away from hungry niggaz," she said with laughter.

"Ok…Ok…this you, little miss?" Parker asked.

I nodded in a humbled way, holding back the "Hell yea" that

hid behind my lips. I could see the utter surprise in Parker's face as he said, "Oh, we definitely have to catch up."

We rode until we saw an empty looking restaurant to grab a table. By the time the appetizers had come out, I was totally grossed out by Shantell and Tyson's behavior. Yuck, if they didn't stop groping each other at the table! I really wanted to reach over to Shantell and choke her. She knew I was not feeling the way she was acting all freakish. Luckily, Parker sensed my disease and began to conjure up conversation.

"So what's been up with you? How you out here living Cindy?"

"I'm pretty good Parker. How have you been?"

"Lived 'bout two lives, since I seen you last. Happy to say I'm still living, though."

"I hear you," I said with my eyes saying I totally get you.

Admittingly. I was still a little distracted by how handsome Parker was. He really hadn't aged much at all. In fact, the little boyish look he had when we first met had only matured into a more manly and clean-cut look that worked really well for him. It only felt strange to be talking to him, feeling almost on an even level.

Although we all sat for quite some time, I still was cautious of what I said. Reality was, although Parker seemed cool, I didn't know who he had truly become. And I definitely didn't know this dude Tyson. He just seemed like trouble. I guess he and Shantell's narcissism made perfect company, because two heads that big usually wouldn't fit into small spaces.

We parted ways that night. Shantell could not talk my ear off more about Tyson. I really wanted to drop her off somewhere on the highway, she had my ears burning so much.

"Oh C, I see you and Parker had a little something..something. He's so fine. What's up with that?"

"Girl, don't even go there. That's not happening," I said with a slick grin.

I grinned, but I meant it.

I couldn't decide how I really felt running back into him.

Although I still felt grateful to him for all he had done, I had worked too hard for too long to the past, the past where I'd last seen Parker, behind me. And even though he didn't really mention it, he knew the mud I made it through and I wasn't sure that I really wanted a reminder. Still, Shantell was persistent at selling me on the fact that we should really link with them for business purposes. Me trying to convince her that we were good on our own, seemed to go in one ear and out the other. So like always, I just let her talk.

I guess I had to put my reservations to the side, because I had to admit, I was curious to what these guys had going on. Shantell had started hanging with this dude Tyson more frequently. And when she wasn't with him, she was talking on the phone with him. I did worry that he didn't have that much going on, because seeing how distracted Shantell had been lately, I was sure he had to be slacking also.

I started encouraging Shantell to fall back. Especially if she really wanted to make money with him. But she would hit me with her usual, "I got this C, you know I'm about my money, first and foremost."

I wanted to believe her, but either way, I knew it didn't matter. She'd find some way to justify it anyhow. Her funniest lie was "C, you know I'm just trying to play him close to find out how he moves. I just let him feel like I'm some bimbo chick so he would let down his guard."

I couldn't hold back that laugh, because she knew herself that that was a whole lie. Shantell was all in, even putting me in the middle of it with her baby's father Kimmie. I had to put them all in check, because I had more things on my mind than keeping up with Shantell's alibis. I kept telling her to stop playing with Kimmie. She knew that he was crazy as hell, super possessive and was probably stalking her. Of course Shantell thought she had it all covered. That girl was slick…but she was even more hard-headed.

A NEW FAMILY

Diving deeper into my curiosity lead to Parker and I spending more time together. Well, initially it started with the four of us, but who could ever keep up with Shantell and Tyson?

Spending more time with Parker I understood that he really was not as interested in this lifestyle as I thought he was. He explained he was only trying to help Tyson with a few things since he knew there was really no way of talking Tyson out of the lifestyle he loved so much. All he could possibly offer is some guidance to keep him safe.

"It's dangerous out here," Parker would always say. And I understood all too well what he was talking about.

When I returned back to the city I never imagined I would have been into the things like I am. And I would have never imagined that I would be so fascinated to the point of enjoying it. Life can be so unpredictable.

All the time spent with Parker lead to a close relationship between us. We spent weeks connected at the hip as I showed him New York. He said he couldn't wait to take me to Washington, D.C. where he was from to show me around. I guess since Shantell was caught up in her dangerous love triangle I needed someone to be around and understand me.

I was worried about Shantell's schemes, but she kept brushing me off. No matter how much I warned this girl about her crazy baby's father, she just didn't get it. In fact, "I got this C" is all she would ever say. She even said that when I touched her on her back and she jumped like she was on fire. Obviously, she had taken some very serious punches. She never had to tell me how she got the bruises she had. I had been around Kimmie. I'd seen his jealousy and rage. Shantell could never even be herself around him. She would be quiet as a mouse. Nothing like the Shantell I knew. I told her one time, "when you're ready to ditch this punk, let me know" but she always chose to terrorize herself in the blame game. I loved my girl, sometimes even more than she was loving herself.

Anyways, Parker and I were having fun. Money still was being made but atleast I had some kind of balance. Parker knew all about Lovelle. He held nothing back explaining men to me, which only assured me that my emotional ass had really chased Lovelle away.

The more I kept Parker around, the less I had to think about how pig-headed I was. And after a while it appeared that Parker was living with me. Although it was never expressed verbally, I knew he felt more comfortable around me than at Tyson's house. He complained Tyson kept too much company, and he was tired of hiding his stuff everytime one of these nondescripts were in the house.

Ironically, Parker had such a theory about life that it seemed difficult to believe he was ever so involved in the streets. He often said God spared him death or in jail because he had a greater purpose. While he never said what that purpose was, I could see it in his eyes that whatever it was, he was convinced. Behind his strong silence I could also see that he battled with the consequences of some of the things that he had already done.

Sometimes I thought about it that life we left behind. The life that made us. Who could we have been if we were never subjected to the things that we were? Would we still have met?

I didn't know much about Parker's upbringing. Maybe it was a broken past. Maybe it wasn't. Maybe he was just a rebel. However it was, one thing I knew for certain is that he had somebody praying for him, just like I once had. Maybe this was what was forming the bond that he and I shared.

Being so closely around a man like Parker made me able to strike a comparison. Lovelle was truly the only one that ever had my heart. But he and I had totally different experiences in life, unlike me and Park. This all made me feel vulnerable to his judgement.

I could not even enjoy the moment of him telling me that he loved me, because I felt so ashamed of the things he never knew about me. Could he ever make love to me imagining the Brut and all the faceless sweaty men who murdered my innocence? Would he ever respect a woman who was responsible for selling death by smoke on these streets? How could he, when I was not even sure I could?

Parker showed compassion knowing all the things that I had faced. He had no princess perception of my past, but he hung at my left side like every horrible thing I'd done didn't matter.
Was it reasonable for me that Lovelle could do the same? I just didn't know. And once again how could I ever find out without taking the chance of being hurt again?

I'm such a punk, I thought. Everyday that Lovelle and I didn't speak gave me another day to hide from the ultimate decision I knew I had to make. I trusted that he cared for me, but I knew one day the Love might be on the chopping block.

One night Parker and I stayed up all night talking. The next day we were supposed to ride out to Philly where his children were so he could handle some business and see his family. Parker had been talking real serious about moving to New York. He really had a love for his children's mother and wanted them all to create a new life. I gave my word that I would help them anyway I could.

I had spoken with his children's mother, and I could see why he loved her so much. She was so the contrary to the lifestyle. She wanted her family to have nothing to do with it. I thought it was amazing how much she trusted him. Parker and I spent all this time together and as far as I know, she never got jealous. And I knew for fact that he was indeed worth the trust, because not once did he ever tried to make a move on me. We had a brother and sister type bond forming, one in which I had none other to compare. I felt appreciative that she never interfered in our relationship. Because I was beginning to believe I needed him. And I was at her mercy to share him.

NANA?

We must have talked so long that we fell asleep without even knowing it. Out of nowhere I heard the sound of pots and pans clicking in the kitchen. Astonished by the sound I woke into a dazed state to see what was going on. I looked on the next couch, and there was Parker sleeping, so I knew it wasn't him in our kitchen. I knew I had no rats or mice so this put me at top alert. I reached over and grabbed my little iron bat, and I walked closer to my kitchen. The kitchen light was off to my surprise. So what or who could it be? With fright in my heart I switched on the light ready for combat. But to my surprise, beyond what I could have imagined: there she was. It was Nana.

As real as anything I had ever seen sitting at my table with two pots, just peeling potatoes. She turned around toward me and said, "May-May, pass Nana that celery from out the fridge."

I stood in shock just looking at her, trying to adjust my eyes to what it appeared I was seeing.

"May-May. Baby. The celery. You do still remember where I keep it, don't you?" she said with a half smile.

I don't know why, but I just opened the refrigerator, knelt down and pulled out the celery. I turned around to see her again, and it was so crazy, but the whole kitchen just changed. It was the same kitchen from when I younger. My coloring book still sat next to my favorite seat. The flowers, the curtains, the wallpaper. Even when I looked over to my living room, It too had changed. I heard the sounds of Nana's favorite spirituals play on the record player; only difference, there was no skipping.

"Nana, what are you doing here?" I asked while approaching her with the celery in my hand.

"Making potato salad for church tomorrow, " she answered. "Tomorrow is Pastor's wife birthday…" she started to go on but I interrupted.

"You can't really be here…you're not here…you're not alive."

Nana then lifted her head up toward me, placed the knife and the potato she'd been skinning on the table. She stood up, and what was weird was the fact that she was not wearing the house-coat and rollers she just was in; she now was wearing the pretty white dress that I remembered we buried her in. I never forgot how she looked when I said my last goodbye. Some said that it would be too traumatic for me to have remembered that, but no matter what, without a picture or anything, I never forgot. She smiled and reached for my face.

"You sent for me chile, didn't you?"

"What?" I asked.

Then I thought for a moment. Suddenly I remembered my dream when I slid a note under her door.

"Nana, how did you get it? I…"

"Now May-May," she responded. "I always heard you. I already heard your heart before it could turn into words. I love you, Baby."

My eyes then began to cry out, hearing words like only my Nana could speak. She wiped my tears as she pulled me into her embrace.

"It's alright, It's alright…let it go," she repeated as I sobbed uncontrollably in her bossoom.

I cried out, "Please stay, Nana, Please stay!"

I hadn't cried out in need of anyone in my life like I cried out to my Nana. It's like she knew everything I was going through and was squeezing the pain out of me. I held her tightly until she pulled away.

"Now, May-May never forget what your Nana has put in you. You know my hopes for you. And no matter what happened, you know who you truly are. You are light and I need you to never forget this." I nodded in agreement. "Don't take your eyes off God, little Cindy Maze. That's who has been keeping you. That's who keeps all of my babies. I don't want to see you getting in that blue car either."

"What car, Nana?" I asked her. Confused, because I knew no one with a blue car.

"Be careful, May-May. The devil trying offer you a ride you may never get off. Just..." Just then she began to take a face of being ill.

"What's wrong, Nana?"

She gave me this tired look and said, "Oh, nothing baby. I just have to sit down."

I pulled her seat so that she could sit down. "Do you need something, Nana?"

"No, No baby. I got Jesus, that's all I need. But back to you, Princess. Everything is going to be OK. All you need is the faith of a mustard seed. And that ain't a lot, baby. Just hold on..."

And just like that before my eyes she changed back into the same house coat from moments earlier.

"Now baby, pass your Nana some of that mayo over there."

I turned to get the mayonnaise, but when I turned back it was only in time enough to see a gleaming light turn into darkness. I wiped my eyes twice, not wanting to let go of the sight of my Nana. My heart wept as I pleaded from the inside for her to return. "God, don't do this," I cried. I shut my eyes to only wake again laid across the couch with pillows spread everywhere. And Parker right across on the next couch.

I sat up for a minute. Still slightly in a daze but feeling the physical feeling of being hit by a truck. I stood up, walked into the bathroom and turned on the lights. Right at this moment I realized I was truly awake. I looked at my swollen eyes in the mirror. Face still moistened by tears, while I asked, What was that all for? Was that the last time I will ever see Nana?... and why did it feel so real?

I took myself to my bedroom and laid across my bed. I had never felt so exhausted by sleep in my life. I Let time pass until the sun gazed brightly through the shades on my window. I had so much on my mind. I heard Parker watching television in the living room so I knew he was up and ready to make moves.

"Cindy, what's the plan for today?"

"I don't know. It's Sunday, I kind of want to go hit up a church or something."

"What you gone' stick a church up?" Parker said jokingly.

"No Butthole, I want to sit in the dang place and pray like the other people. Stop playing," I responded laughingly.

"You wanna go?" I asked.

"Naw, I was just thinking. I can go to Philly on the way back. I need to go tie up some loose ends in Washington before I go."

"Wow. Park....You know I would have rode to Philly. That's right here, but I I have some things out here you know I need to handle."

"Yea, I know. Just checking," he said.

"Could we ride out Wednesday? I will be good then."

"Naw, it's alright, C. Handle your handle. I will be back by then. You know that talk we had last night really got me ready. We gotta pursue this plan. No kidding around. Besides, Tyson and Shantell ready to sweep town. I heard Shantell's real man was on some other stuff last night. Your girl tryna get away for a little cool down."

"What Park, what happened?'

"You know it's none of my business, and I'm damn sure not saying Tyson is any better; but you really need to talk to your girl."

"I hear you, Park. You know I be trying but…"

Just then we heard a honking outside. Parker looks out the window and said, "These crazy…"

I knew it had to be Shantell and Tyson. They just held no regard when they were together. Bright Sunday morning and they'll be in front of your house blasting vulgar music acting crazy. I just shook my head. I let a minute or two go before I heard my intercom ring. It was my sweet and meek friend, Shantell.

Yea, right. It was my obnoxious friend yelling through the speaker "hurry up, let's roll out."

"I'm not going with y'all Shantell. You know its things that need to be handled."

"Why don't you send Scrap or one of them to do it? You totally are not taking advantage of being a Boss C. Lighten up."

Shantell had me thinking for a moment. I probably could have passed this off, but I was just so particular in the ways I liked things handled. I thought to myself: C, just go. What the worst that could happen in just a few days?

Parker looked at me to see that I was slightly unsure what I wanted to do. "Cindy, you riding?" he asked.

"I don't know Park, should I?"

"Well you know my answer will always be to do what you think is best for you first. But you know I would feel better if I didn't have to deal with them two knuckleheads by myself."

I laughed a bit already understanding what he meant. That combo was always full of surprises.

"And looked what they're pulling up in. I guess Tyson ain't trying to put that mileage on his car, and neither is your girl. Take a look."

I walked over to the window and looked out. And to my shock they were leaning on a mint-condition navy blue Acura. Immediately my mind went to a panic.

"Naw Park, Y'all can't go! Y'all can't go! Something's not right!" Park watched as I went into a slight hysteria.

"What…what are you saying? C, are you okay?"

"No Park, I had a dream about this. My Nana came to me in my sleep and told me not to ride in this blue car. I'm serious Park. Don't do it!"

Parker looked at me, first with concern then assurance. Just then the intercom rang. This time it was Tyson.

"Y'all coming down or what, Cuz?"

Parker looked over to me and then answered. "Yo, Cindy has this bad vibe. Maybe we should hold up on this trip for a second."

"Man stop playing! Tell Cindy stop playing. You talk me into riding out. Me and Shantell move everything over for you and you coming with this?"

Parker looked back over to me as he saw my defeated expression. "He's right C. Everything is going to be okay. I will back before you know."

I shook my shoulders in frustration. For the first time, Parker and I were on total different scopes of this situation. And I knew it was no use trying to convince Shantell because whatever Tyson was on, I knew she would agree. She'd been like that lately.

"Whatever, y'all be careful. I'll see you when you get back." I said with as much nonchalance as I could pretend.

Parker grabbed his gym bag and went for the door. Before he left, he gave me a deep stare. "Cindy, you going to church right? Pray for us. And remember we have important things to do when I get back. You just be ready, Princess."

Parker had never called me Princess before. And it immediately put my mind back to my dream last night where my Nana called me Princess.

"Don't worry Park, I am just tripping. Everything will be alright," I said with a half smile.

Parker left and I just sat for a moment. I heard the car pull off as the music faded.

"Cindy, what are you going to do today?" I asked myself. I walked into the bedroom, opened both of my closet doors and just sat on my bed staring at my clothes. Boy did I have a lot of them. Designers, designers, designers all draped my closet. But believe it or not, I didn't find anything I felt appropriate to go to church. It's not like I needed to have a big church hat or something, I just didn't want to stand out like a sore thumb.

Well I sat until I totally talked myself out of going altogether. Ten thirty and I was still sitting on my bed. God knows our hearts, my Nana used to say. He was just going to have to know it today, I thought.

HIS LIFE, MY HANDS

I took the remainder of the Sunday to relax. I guess I had worked myself up so much emotionally, I didn't want to do too much afterward. I went out to grab some take-out and came right back to lounge on my couch. It had been some time since I had been in the house by myself, and I knew what I really needed was to sit down with my thoughts for awhile.

The only call I made was to Scrap to make sure he and Pope would be ready for tomorrow. In this game everybody had to have them a Scrap or Pope. I ran across these two young guys by way of connect. They were little hot-headed thugs when I met them, but put a man in some nice threads and give them a mission, and well, little businessmen had formed.

Still hot headed and trigger happy, but just more disciplined. They only had to put in minor work since they got with us. Mostly bodyguard type work, but they both had reputations that preceded them. I didn't care to know everything they had done, as long as they stayed focused and dedicated when around me.

After everything was set up right, I was cool to relax my mind. Sure my thoughts wandered over to Shantell, Parker and Tyson every once in awhile. But for the most part it was brainless activity for me at that point.

Sleep fell on me and before I had knew it, the next day had come.

I got myself ready, gave myself my usual boss talk in the mirror, and headed out. My poker face had improved so much over the years. I always looked over-serious and intense while handling business. I knew one slip up could get me hit.

Jealousy was all around me. The ones that praised me the most, scared me the most. I knew any one of them was just waiting for my downfall. I was making the game look too easy. So keeping my guard up was a must.

I hit the spot waiting for the drop just as dust fell from the sky. Sunlight was gone and the whole dynamic of the streets was switching up. All the real vampires, as I would call them, were out. Children and working people knew when to clear the streets for this life to begin. Only thing in my eye's view, were petty dealers, street walkers and fiends.

Usually it would be me, Shantell and some protection waiting in the car for these type of situations, but this evening I sat solo waiting for the other car to drive up. I still felt pretty safe though. Scrap and Pope stood posted on opposite corners observing from every angle. I watched them, my rearview mirror and the clock. It wouldn't be long until this thing was on and over with.

I took my eyes off everything for a minute to place my bag in the glove compartment when I heard a thump on my back passenger side mirror. A body stood off to the side of the pavement seeming to be trying to get my attention. I turned my radio down even lower to hear a dry and groggy voice ask, "You got something?... You got something?"

With the dust of night I couldn't quite make out the face since my car sat pretty low, but the odor invaded my car space as I slightly lowered my window.

It was a junky. And before I could see his face clearly it was apparent that half of his right arm was missing.

"Get the hell away from here!" I yelled as he continued to mutter in a doped out voice, "What you got man? I need some."

At this time I could see scrap and pope moving in closer. I could tell they were contemplating blowing cover over this fiend. But like I said, these boys stayed ready for anything.

I rolled down my window more to make sure this drug addict could hear me clearly as I told him no and all in one moment two things happened. The champagne-colored car I was waiting on blinked and rode right pass me and the addict knelt his face directly at my passenger side window.

What came next I was in no way prepared for. As me and this man locked eyes intensely, I realized I knew him and he knew me. It was Big Richie.

"Cindy?" he said with his face now looking sobered up but frightened. "Is that you?" he asked.

Before I knew it like I time bomb my emotions exploded.

"Motherfucker…You bitch ass, Mother…" I spurted out my mouth as my my body emerged out of the driver seat and already around to the passenger side where he stood backing up against my car. I popped my truck open to get out my little faithful bat, and when the street light hit the gleam of my silver hitter, that's when the whole environment changed. His friends all ran toward us. Lights went on in windows of apartment and Scrap and Pope came running over.

Big Richie who once stood like a giant to me was this feeble looking dirty man slipping against my car with no defense.

"Cindy no," he cried as I lifted my bat to strike the first time.

"You know me, don't cha? You want something from me, huh? I got what you're looking for," I taunted him with rage in my voice.

I felt my wrist vibrate as the swing of the bat met harshly against his bones. I went berserk and was totally unaffected by his plea. Scrap and Pope, seeing how I was handling the situation, gave me a look of confusion as they cleared the crowd and encouraged everyone to walk off and mind their own business. I yelled to them to stay back as I continued to swing at Big Richie's hunched over body on the concrete, as he was whimpering, "I'm sorry Cindy, so sorry."

The memory played in my mind in quick flashes of this man that I once trusted. The man who sold me to death. I had waited years for this moment and it had finally brought about the revenge I had longed for. My body had picked up the rhythm of my swing as my mind went totally absent. I knew that fatal blow was coming soon to this man who had nowhere to run or fight back.

It was the sound of a child's voice screaming "Nana...Nana, please come upstairs" that brought me back. This is just when I heard sirens in the distance and snapped out of my rage. Scrap pulled the bloodied bat from my clench as they yelled at me to come on.

I still heard Big Richie's voice cry, "I'm sorry, Cindy" through the commotion as I left him motionless on the curb. I was pushed into the back seat of my car as Pope sped off like a race car driver in my vehicle. In perfect timing though, I looked back in the distance to see the spotlights of police vehicle at the scene.

"What the hell was that, yo?" Scrap asked. Having no clue of how deep-seated and long-awaited moment that was. For the first time I felt the darkness in me. And I knew just then...something had to change.

The boys got me home safe, but I was still a little pissed that I missed out on my money.

Sympathy for what I had just done hadn't completely arrived. I just felt the soreness of my own joints as I sat with everything from my heart to my legs pumping hard.

It took awhile until I was in a regular mind-state. I then started to think of what I had done, and knew I just needed to talk to someone. My first thought was Lovelle. I dismissed that with a Hell no, are you crazy girl! He will think you were an animal.

Added to this fact was the reality that I would have to tell him the whole back story. Nope. Next… Shantell, Parker: both no answer. Rudy: no answer. Finally I was tapped out. It was just me alone facing these demons. I had never felt so scared of myself before.

THE CALL

I was totally exhausted. I slept in for a whole day trying to clear my mind of what I had faced. I went in between emotions. Seeing Big Richie's face flash back and forth between the clean cut debonaire man I once knew as a child to the mangled, drug-abused man with one arm.

I knew it was totally wrong to beat on someone that was near defenseless, but I felt he had it coming. I trusted him at one point of my life. And that was always something I was scared to do. He betrayed me and sold me like a slave. What else was I supposed to do? I guess karma is a bitch.

I moved around my house for a while until I realized there was nothing I wanted to eat in the house. I figured I go grab a bite to eat and than go to my nail salon and get one of them ladies to give me a quick little massage. If that didn't work, I knew I might have to go to the hospital to check if I had sprained something and I definitely didn't want to do that!

As I was just about to grab my keys, the phone rang. At first it only rang once, but when I picked up there was just the sound of a dial tone. But just as I started to look through the caller ID, it rang again and strange number popped up. Usually I would have waited until someone left a message, but something told me to pick up.

A woman's voice that I kind of recognized said "Hello?"

"Hey, who's this?" I asked.

"Hi, C. It's me: Lisa. Parker's girl. How you doing?"

I noticed her voice was a little more monotone than I remembered.

"Hey Lisa, What's going on? Have you heard from Parker? Is he with you?" I let my questions come out all in one breath.

"C, that's why I'm calling you. I've been in the hospital with Parker for the past three days."

I interrupted in an instant panic. "What? Why is he in the hospital? What happened? Where's Shantell?"

Lisa let me jumble my reaction into a quick interrogation and then she began to tell me what happened. There had been an altercation at a gas station, not far from where she lived. She, Parker, Tyson and Shantell were paying for their things at the counter when some guys walked in the store. One of the guys pushed between them to throw two dollars for whatever he was taking and accidently made Shantell spill her drink on herself. He did apologize, but Tyson and Shantell began to curse him and his friends out until one of the guys left the store and told them to come outside. Parker told her to wait inside as he followed behind to try to defuse the situation and moments later shots rang out.

It all happened so fast she said. One minute they were paying for their snacks and the next Parker was lying on the ground with a shot to the head. Tyson was laid across Shantell's lap with blood coming from everywhere and Shantell appeared to be shot in the back of her leg with scuffs and scratches from her fall.

It was all too much to take in for me. Lisa began to give me full account of the situation as I stood shaking with tears.

"C, don't worry, just pray for Parker. He's doing the worst. Doctors have been working intensely on him and have put him into an induced coma until they can remove the debris from his head. They say he should not lose any function if all goes well. I always said Parker was hard headed. I guess it played in his favor this time." I knew she said to lighten my mood.

"I hear you Lisa, but what about Shantell and Tyson?"

"Tyson should be released tomorrow or the day after. Shantell, I picked up yesterday. She's resting and taking that medication they gave her. She's really shaken up. She said she couldn't get through to you. As frantic as she was, she probably was dialing the wrong number. But everything is everything as long as Parker pulled through."

I sighed in relief. "Where exactly are y'all at. I'm coming."

"No, C, I know you want to, but there is really no reason to come this far. We are all heading that way once this is all said and done. I promise to call you if I feel something has taken a turn. I really promise!" she said.

Lisa had a calm disposition similar to my Nana it seemed. The way she was handling tending to everyone by herself confirmed the reasons why Parker would choose her and start the family that they had. I trusted what she told me but it didn't stop me from worrying. I told her to have Shantell call me and keep me posted.

After we hung up, my mind and spirit felt the exhaustion of having run three hundred mile races. I was scared, and this was a feeling that I didn't like to feel. Everyone that I had was nowhere to talk me through it either. What was I going to do? Figure this out C, I said to myself.

I sat around the house just watching TV. It was a Thursday afternoon and I needed something. I thought about going to have a drink at a bar, but I just couldn't see myself getting drunk with no one around to watch me. I knew that Bizet and Scrap were totally confused by me after the other night, so I wanted to give them some cool down time.

My mind went in several different directions. I couldn't imagine what was going through Parker's mind at the time. We would always discuss the possibility of his past catching up with him.

There had always been a lingering concern that the partners he cut ties with would come back to wage war. But never did we consider this random situation occurring. All these thoughts scared me and I really did not want to be alone.

It would have been nice to check on the Dawsons, but it had been so long since I had spoken with one of them, they probably would have looked at me like I was crazy. I thought of all of this as I flickered through the channels.

Somehow I stumbled across this cable access channel. On the TV was a minister speaking. It was a live program that was going on. From the looks of people finding seats, he must have just begun speaking. I sat for a while and listened. Hearing both this minister and my conscience speak, I felt an unusual urge to be sitting in the midst of these people, just as I gave myself all the justifications to why I should just sit on my couch.

"It's not Sunday girl, you can go to church on Sunday like you planned. You don't have nothing to wear, and besides you don't know where you going."

A flash of words passed by on the bottom of the screen and the minister began to invite the viewers to come as they are, out to this all night worship service. As I read the screen I was totally shocked that this church was less than ten minutes away. In fact, I knew exactly where it was although I never walked in. "C, just go!" I told myself.

I got up before I had another moment to talk myself out of it. Before I knew it I was driving myself right to the front of the place I was just watching from the comfort of my couch. I watched as so many people gathered and walked up these stairs to go in. Men and women, from young to old. Some dressed in jeans, like me, and some with their Sunday best.

I parked and found myself walking in amongst them, hiding behind nothing more than my shades and fedora. I thought to myself, what's the worst that could happen? Parker had always had my back. The least I could do is go in a church and pray for him. My Nana always said that prayers were powerful.

Of course I wanted to sit as close to the door of this big place as possible. But an usher had moved me nearly to the front. I was thinking that with all the people in this church building, I couldn't believe that they'd had the nerve to have a open chair near the front. This had to be a set up.

I know you have to bring lots of money to church, I thought sarcastically. Maybe I could slip one of these old ladies a twenty and they would find me a better seat in the back.

There I went with my messed up mind. "Cindy just get in, so you can get out," I said to myself.

I sat right behind a lady with her two sons. One was a teenager. He looked behind at me as if we were in a prison lock down. His eyes asked, "What are you in for?"

I laughed in my head as I totally understood his feeling as I remembered the three nights a week I went to church with Nana when I was a child. The service was going pretty okay I must admit. Some of these people really could sing, but then as fate would have it, there was a altar call.

I heard everybody start to gather to the front as evangelist Cecili Johnson prayed us out of service. "Okay Cindy," I said to myself. "Just follow this crowd, and it would be all over soon." I lingered behind the people that which gathered at the front of the church. Heck, no matter what they say about church folk, some folks were pushing each other to move closer. If you didn't know better, you would have thought somebody was giving away something for free.

But just by random placement I found myself sifted around until I actually wound up being one of the people standing dead center to where the Evangelist walked over and stood. As she stared over the sea of believers, I couldn't help but to find the irony of the situation. "Cindy, bring it in…focus," I said to myself. "Concentrate on Parker. That's who you're here for."

I put my best effort toward relaxing. I realized if I didn't totally relax my mind, there was nothing holding me from busting a U-turn and getting out of this church. I took my last look around me, then I shut my eyes. With nothing distracting to see I found myself more in tune with the organ that played.

I have to say, whoever was playing that thing was talented. Was it wrong for me to be thinking: why are they hiding their talent in here? Anyways, I was probably dead wrong for thinking this. Cindy focus!...

Humming, loud crying, the amens and hallelujahs were already beginning to fill the place. I wondered what was taking the preacher or evangelist so long to begin. Not to be rude, but I was starting to feel I was at a pre-show. But just in the nick of time she began to speak.

At first it seemed like she was speaking a language I had never heard but then she began to cry out "She has been abandoned Father. Your child is lost and nearly forgotten. You know her bruises from the inside out. She is here today Lord. Claim back your child!"

At hearing this, I was totally drawn in. A warm feeling began to set on my eyes as the voice became more and more bold. Who in here could she be talking about? Why does it seem that they lived the same life that I had?

"She is Yours....She is yours," she cried out. Suddenly I felt a hand touching and holding my forehead. Strangely, as she held my head, prayers rapidly falling from her lips. A feeling I had never felt in my life fell over me. With every word of prayer, and with the now resounding out crying of the congregation, my eyes rained warm tears. With every word of prayers I felt the electricity. I felt my pain and anguish heat my skin and I hoped once she removed her hand from me the pain and memories will leave with her. I was overtaken, I spaced out... At this moment, I was not amongst anyone else. I was not the hesitating women who snuck into the church and camouflaged herself amongst believers. It was weird, but not weird enough for me to want to escape the feeling. I heard a thunderous voice that was deep into my ears as I zoned into this emotion. It was not the evangelist anymore…it was something else. It was a sound that was more like thunder. It said no word audibly yet my soul responded to every vibration. I felt a plea inside of me, I heard my sub-conscience ask Could it be you?

Without feeling my feet on the ground, I became totally entrenched by this outer-worldly experience. I heard an intense deep-drumming voice say, "My Child" and without any reservation, I knew for certain it was Him.

In some tunnel of my consciousness I knew this was the voice that I secretly yearn to hear. Shortly after, a high pitch ding resounded in my ear like when the networks do testing on the television. Images raced through my head flash by flash until finally I broke through to my consciousness.

And where was I but laid out on the floor with ushers holding my hands gazing down at me. What the heck? I questioned as my thoughts gathered. How did I get on this floor?... Who pushed me? I struggled for a second to get up while a little lady I had never seen before wiped my face with a white cloth. My face was soaked from eyelids to nostrils. I know I looked a mess but that was the least of my concern because as I was helped me to my feet I felt as light as a feather. My legs felt like spaghetti and it seemed even brighter in the church. This had never happened in church. This had never happened to me. This was beyond what my imagination could conjure. I'd been touched. By what? It must have been God because Cindy, makes no spectacle of herself by no human affect at all.

Home from church I felt no need to do much. I just sat on my couch pondering what this all could have meant. I can't say I was worried or anything. In fact, the mysticism of the days experience occupied my whole thought. I asked: now what? What happens to me now? What am I supposed to do about it? But I didn't hear that voice say anything toward any of my questions. "Great," I said. As if I hadn't enough questions for it. Now a new list, fantastic.

Suddenly I broke out of my spell. Gotta call Shantell. Well didn't have to consider it long because my phone rang right at the thought. One thing for certain, I didn't want to hear drama and by the yell of excitement from the other side of the line. I was please to assume that there was none.

"C! Girl what you doing?" Shantelle blurted excitedly.

"Nothing girl, just getting in."

"Well C, somebody wants to talk to you."

"Where are you Shantelle ? Who is it?" I asked.

After a short pause I heard a male voice say "What's up, Youngin'?"

"Parker!" I yelled "What's up? how are you?"

"I had a little accident Hahahahaha," he replied.

"You crazy Parker, but I'm glad to hear your voice. You scared the mess out of me!"

"Yeah I know, C, but I'm okay."

"But what about Tyson?" I asked.

"He's good, he gets out today."

"That sounds good, real good! But when am I going to see you?"

"Soon Cindy, real soon. Plan still must go on."

I knew exactly what he was talking about when he said "The Plan." We said our goodbyes, although I was surprised "The Plan" was still on his mind after this all occurred. I mean even revenge would have been one of my first thoughts after this all happened. Obviously "The Plan" was even more significant to Parker now that he had escaped with his life. I guess there was not too much more you could ask for.

Well one thing for sure, I thought, today was a day! I didn't know where God was a couple of years ago but obviously he found time for me on that day because Parker was alright and that was all that mattered to me. Thank God, I thought. Thank God!!!!!!!

147

I could go on and on about the weeks and months that followed. Besides Parker's path to recovery and Shantell's drama, I was too consumed with everyone else's life to get into my own. My run with the streets had decreased, partly because my wants had changed and partly because the police activity had increased.

Speaking of police activity, there had been a van across the street from my apartment for a while. I inquired about it, but no one gave me any type of satisfactory answers. I started to believe it was not abandoned. Shantell always said I was paranoid. I just called it being cautious. Usually when my vibes weren't right about something, I was dead on.

Anyways, I moved through these weird occurrences watching who called me and what they said over the phone. Also, I never conducted any business too close to home. Wish I could have said that for Shantell. I really don't know what had gotten into her. It seemed like ever since Tyson was shot and she'd been creeping taking care of him, she'd been more weird than ever. A couple of times I had to put her in her place. True, she was the one who introduced me to the game and without her my status wouldn't have been where it was now, but she was starting to act more like an intern than a partner. Louder, flashier and careless. Not to mention telling too much of our business to Tyson. Injured or not, I always felt Tyson was real suspect. Those bullets hadn't put not one ounce of sense in his head and if I hadn't known any better, I would have said they made him even more greasier than before.

Tyson said, Tyson said, Tyson said, all she knows is what Tyson said. It is crazy how independent woman retire their own will for love. But besides that, something was weighing heavier than ever on me. Even though I stood in judgement of Shantell, the truth was I still missed Lovelle with all of my heart.

I spoke with him a few times. Nothing over-the-top but just minor conversations about our days about. Sure, we would try to talk about us, but that always lead to somebody hanging up.

I kid you not, those international charges were no joke to my phone bill.

I asked all of the things an ex-girlfriend who was still in love would. Like has he moved on, how was his sex life, and all of that. But I could never get too much out of him; he would only ask the same questions back to me. He even hinted I was involved with Parker but I just figured that was to distract me from what he was really doing. If I had learned nothing more as being a woman, I learned never tell a man about your male friends. Suspicion will always give way.

Women talk too much! I needed to control myself, especially my mouth! Besides that I had a lot of figuring out to do. With Parker and I constantly speaking about our plans, the thought of my brother began to become forefront in my thoughts. I had almost forgotten my initial intentions for coming back into the city. I guess over time, I opted to avoid the mission because it brought a lot of emotion to the forefront, like my feelings about Big Richie and of course my mother.

Twelve years had passed and a lot of story in between since I'd last seen Boo. I didn't quite know the lifespan for crackheads and drug dealers, so my expectation to see anyone other than Little Richie was fading. After all this time, I had no idea what he would look like, where he'd been or even if he would remember me. Sometimes I even thought that maybe I might be doing Little Richie a favor by leaving his life alone. You see, life doesn't always imitate fiction. Sure I could go and play hero, tell him the hell that I've been through to find him. But what would happen next? Would we escape to a castle in the sky? You see, movies make it so simple. Hero saves the day right? But it never shows the day after. Could we ever be sure that our day after will be something to look forward to? I mean I had a lot of work to do if that was ever going to happen.

In the middle of all this worry, a thought popped in my head Cindy get away for a minute! And with no job, family or responsibilities that seemed exactly the right thing to do. A quiet week away. Maybe I could get myself together. To be really honest, I was tired of everything. I needed to get away from the apartment and even all of the paranoia. So that's what I did. I didn't travel anywhere too far, actually I just went to this place called the Poconos, somewhere out in Pennsylvania.

This get away was just what I needed. A hot tub, spa treatment, maybe even a book. Soon after settling in, the time away from the congestion of the city began to have an effect on me. It felt the closest to being perfect.

I was on the deck overlooking a poolside where I figured out my biggest problem. I was unhappy. Yes, I had money to do whatever I wanted, even enough to take a getaway a few times year, but in reality I had nothing! No love, no family. Just shoes, clothes and pocketbooks. Besides awful memories and secrets, the type of secrets that has me sitting at a beautiful resort alone, I measured myself as broke and broken.

If I really felt wishing could make a difference, I would have wished Lovelle was here, sipping pina coladas and enjoying this view. But the only thing that plagued my thoughts was the fact that I had never met a man that could love me and my secrets. I hoped Lovelle would be that man, but how vulnerable would I have to become in order to find out if he could really love all of me?

For a moment, in the midst of all that appeared beautiful, I wanted to just let it all end. I played with the thought of controlling my own destiny, letting it all go, and for the first in a long time not let life just happen to me. I wondered what was on the other side of all this pain that I had seen throughout my life. But, it was only just a thought. I knew that would have been quitting. and I may have been many things, but a quitter I was not!

Instead I chose to take in the peace of the day. Appreciate the fact that this was more than just a stolen moment. I began to see this time as a opportunity to reflect. To ask the right questions, like…Who was Cindy Maze?

There is a lot wrapped up in the question of "Who?" It connotes honesty, identification, depth! Clearly I had been through so much in my years, that somehow I just lost my "Who."Yet, I did know what I was. I was a great pretender, a lost child and enemy to myself. I wondered how was it that I escaped captivity only to be locked into an even more confined existence? When did I stop fighting to be free and new? or had I ever really fought at all?

The knock of room service distracted my deep thinking, and luckily too, because I think I was going to ask myself the wrong question and be deeper in confusion than I already was. One thing for certain, I may not have known everything about who I was, but whoever my "who" was, she really loved seafood!

CHANGE IN THE AIR.

A change of pace occurred shortly after my hiatus. The quiet storms of my emotions subsided and I felt I was just at the brink of discovering who Cindy Maze was or had forgotten to be. Money still flowed without much of my effort, but something in me had changed.

I had often complained about being lonely, but for once it was what I preferred. I had visits every now and again from Parker and Shantell, but other than that I stayed outside of the limelight. I kissed a few frogs during this time, but there still was only one kiss that I missed.

I had heard through the Grapevine that Lovelle would be returning soon, and although he and I had become cordial over time, I doubted he would return with the same heart for me. Actually, in the midst of our later conversations, he actually admitted to dating someone in Canada.

He said that it was nothing serious, but I figured if it were worth a mention, especially to me, it had to mean something. My pride kept me from crying about it, but believe me I wanted to. Usually I would try to sedate the feeling with shopping, but I had to admit that was starting to get expensive.

So instead of shopping, playing the streets or sulking on the couch, I got out there in a good way. I even started talking to some folks about setting into a proper business. I always heard that real estate was the way to go. I heard of plenty of people in my line of business that made the investment. Maybe I could be the face on one of them corny billboards at the bus stops.

While I hated to bring everything back to Lovelle, I could see him finding me in a sexy business suit and briefcase attractive. That was enough of a motivation for me. I needed to get a new me going quickly. The last thing I needed was him coming back and hearing what I'm really about out here. A proper business man with a dope dealing princess, might not be the move to get me to true happiness. If I knew how to do nothing else, I knew how to adjust

Although I had workers and my face was rarely seen, I still had people who were jealous of me. I could name a list that would find it delightful to mess up anything that they thought would make me happy, my relationships included.

Even with no legitimate education and no job, I still maintained the lifestyle of a 5th Avenue woman. I started to guess it was just time to make that all add up. One plus one, should always equally two. If not something was definitely wrong.

RANDOM

Talk about a random call. I received a message from a man claiming to have some really important information for me. He left a time and a meeting place but no call back number, or reference to what the information was pertaining to. I called Parker over to my apartment to listen to the message. We both agreed that it sounded like an older cat. And the fact that he knew my whole name and how to find me because I wasn't listed made us even more interested. If anyone knew me by my original name, they would have had to known me in my childhood. Everyone called me C. I was so careful that I was even reluctant to give my name to the people I'd been considering doing business with. Street snakes and cooperate snakes might look different, but all of them still crawl. I never let myself forget this.

The meeting time with this stranger was for the following day, and the address was only vaguely familiar. In fact, I didn't recognize the address at all. Parker was no help either. He knew less about the city than I had. But just as protective as he always is, he volunteered to go along with me.

I didn't like to do things like this. I waited and waited for this man to call again, but he didn't. I wondered why would someone contact me and not call to actually speak to me over the phone?

This was suspicious, maybe even a little bit dangerous, but it did make me curious.

Hope it wasn't what they said about curiosity: you know how it be killing cats. Cause if so, I was one dead cougar.

The next day I arose to find Parker already dressed, looking like he had stayed up the whole night through.

"Parker, Whats up?" I asked.

"Naw C, I'm cool. Just thinking about what we are getting into for the day".

"What, the meeting?''

"Yeah, I don't know C. Should I bring something with us?''

"Something like what, Park? If you don't feel safe, I understand. I know what you've gone through!"

"Yeah right, like I'm really about to let you face some Magnum P I ish alone" he smirked." You really think you're Mega Woman, don't you?"

"Naw Park, you never know, this could be a money move. I'm more anxious than scared.''

"Well, Treasure…"

"Hey, What's with that? Treasure's dead. What you bringing her up for?'' I asked with a look of disappointment.

"No, no offense" he said. "It's just that you get so gangster at times. Like how you were back then."

"Careful, Parker. That name digs up a lot for me," my voice crackled. I knew he meant no harm, but just the mention of that name brought back anger that I had suppressed for a long time.

"My bad C, poor choice of words."

"No doubt, Park. No harm, no foul. Are you still willing to go?"

"You know me C. Just let me know how we doing this."

I was relieved that he had not changed his mind. I know sometimes I'm independent to fault, but there are times I really need someone.

"Think I should take a cab, and you could take my car. that way you can post up somewhere and be vigilant just in case something is not right."

"I got you C, I will tailgate. You can call me if you have some feeling or a change in plan, cool?"

I agreed. That's why I loved Parker. Although he was protective, he was not overbearing. Something like an older brother that I never had. He was street smart, so I knew that even if he caught a bad vibe he would be first to check me.

I rode in the taxi once it came, and I noticed Parker was no further than a car behind. My stomach was still a little tight at the fact that I didn't know exactly what I was heading into. But I figured, what all really go on in such a early part of the day? It's funny how the unexpected can bring forth so many mixed emotions. I admit, I didn't have nothing, but nothing is still a lot to lose.

Anyhow, before I knew it the driver said "This is it."

I was thrown off. The building looked like a clinic or nursery. I jumped out of the car, looked around and checked for Parker. Parker had himself park on the far corner and he flickered his light to let me know he was watching.

The block was quiet and I stayed close to the curb, instantly becoming impatient waiting for this man to show himself. I looked at all the corners expecting to see him arrive but to my surprise, right behind me the door to the building opened, and a mid aged man approached.

" I thought I saw you out here, why didn't you come inside?" he asked.

I looked at him baffled.

"Excuse me, aren't you Cindy?' he asked.

"Yes, and I take it that you the one who called."

"Yes, I would be him. You may come inside. It is safe! I will tell you everything you need to know."

He then put his arms across my shoulder and guided me inside. He didn't look intimidating. In fact, he wore a Muslim-styled beanie on his head and a buttoned down collared shirt. I laughed to myself thinking, If this was some Gangsta stuff, the game surely had changed its Em O.

Mid-thought my cell phone buzzed from Parker, but I sent it to voicemail; hopefully letting him know I was cool. I observed my surroundings and realized I was in some youth center of some sort. It seemed like a YMCA. I watched as young kids walked around, some slapping five to this man and all together I was even more confused. This was the last thing I expected from this meeting.

The man then guided me to what seemed like an office I took it as being his own because of the many plaques that were around and how comfortably he sat behind the big oak desk.

I broke the formality with, "What's up? What's this all about?"

I felt like I was at the meeting with my principal for a second. And still this man gave me no name I thought to myself.

"Who are you?" I asked with suspicious eyes. "What did you call me for?"

He just sat across from me with a really intense stare. It was like he was studying me, but I can't say it was in lustful type of manner. Finally he spoke.

"Cindy, I know you don't know me, I feel I may have some information that may be interesting to you." I postured my body to show I was listening closely, but face still showed unenthused.

"Cindy, my name is Jesse. They call me Mr. J around here at the center. I work with inner city kids that either have noone viable to mentor them or have different sets of issues."

"Ok," I said, sort of sarcastically. "Well listen Jesse, J, Mr. J, whomever. Let's get to the point, can't we?' I don't like the way you called me to her like this was some kind of covert mission and you've already taken up valuable time!" I knew I was extra blunt, but this all made no sense to me. Just as I was saying this, Parker walked right in behind me.

"Excuse me, may I help you?" Jesse asked.

"Everything's straight?" Parker asked me.

"I'm fine, Mr. Jesse here was just getting to the point. Weren't you, Mr. Jesse?"

"Yes, Yes… Let me just tell you! I have been in this field of rec for over fifteen years and over the last three years I have had the pleasure of overseeing a young man by the name of Richard."

" I have a brother by that name," I jumped to in response.

" I know." Jesse said.

"He has been at me to find you for a very long time. And as promised, here we are."

I turned my head toward Parker as Jesse continued to explain in the background of sound. I couldn't believe it. I wanted to cry, but I was too in shock from what I was hearing.

I looked at Parker as he squeezed my hand and listened. I turned back at Mr. Jesse, right as he asked me if I was interested in being reunited with Richard.

"Of course, why wouldn't I?" I asked.

Mr. Jesse then went on to explain that Richard had weathered a tremendous amount of disappointments so far in his life, and he didn't want him to have to endure any further.

"No, no, Mr. Jesse. I understand, but I would never…That's my little Bro."

He explained to us that Little Richie had spent some time in the foster care system, and had been shifted around for a couple of years, but he felt it would be excellent if he had been in contact with those who were biological family. I asked had Little Richie been adopted and he said, "No, not really."

Maybe I should have asked more questions but really the only thing that was on my mind was when I was going to see my Little Boo again.

Once he let me know that it could be arranged in a couple of days, I felt a sense of relief.

Leaving the center I knew life as I had known it would change. As random as it occurred, and as ready as I always thought I was, I began to realize I was nervous. And the panic set in.

I mean, Richie Boo was now a teenager. I didn't know what that might be like. I just knew that it should never be like mine had been.

The good news is that he remembered me. I remember so many days of playing with him and his trucks, promising to one day ride him in a real one. Sweet memories, but the anxiety came from wondering, what if he had questions? What if he thought I left him? How could I explain? How much would be too much for him to handle?

Well, while all of these thoughts pondered in my head I hadn't really paid any attention to Parker, whom had a really bizarre look on his face as well.

"Whats up, Park?" I asked.

"I'm cool," he said in his usual reserved tone.

"Can you believe this, Park? I mean should I believe this guy?"

"C, the truth is, he seems upright. The question now is more so, What has to happen now?"

" I know, Park, I was thinking the same thing. I mean, this is what I've been waiting for, right?"

"Guess so, C. I know there ain't much that you can't handle. You are smart like that!"

"Awe, thanks, Park. That means a lot!"

A NEW TWIST

The day moved slowly after, as I prepared myself for all I knew was to come. I had frequent dreams of myself holding Richie Boo. The only strange thing was that I was grown, but he was still the cute little curly head boy with the illuminating smile that he had when I last saw him..

It seemed like he were my own child in my dream, but I knew in reality things were far different from that. This would be no little boy I would embrace, this would actually be a young man. A young man with a past, a personality and assumingly a lot of questions.

I wondered how much about Big Richie and Denise he would remember. How long had he stayed with them before he was put into the system? Did he resent them the same way I had or did he wish that they would return, the same way that I had at times? I knew there would be a lot to account for, I just hoped that having me would ease some of the pain he and I both shared. The days could not pass quick enough, since it felt I had been waiting forever.

In the midst of wonder, I heard the door knock. As I went to answer it, my phone rang at the same time.

"C", I heard in a piercing high-pitched voice from the other side of the door.

Definitely Shantell.

"Hold on Girl, give me a minute," I yelled as I picked up the phone. "Hello," I answered.

"Hey Missy…" I heard on the other side of the line.

I knew the voice, yet again I said,"Hello" to be for certain all the while I was opening the door for Shantell. She was rambling mid-conversation as usual. I waited to hear the voice on the other side of the line as I signaled for Shantell to hush. Once again the voice on the other side of the phone spoke saying, "Tell Mouth ole Mighty, tongue everlasting to be quiet." I laughed knowing now for sure who it was, Lovelle, no doubt.

"How are you Cindy, I mean Good morning."

Shantell interjected after my greeting and yelled,"Who's that, your husband? Tell Lovelle he better not be saying something slick, I know him."

I laughed knowing nothing has changed in their chemistry since high school. The love/hate relationship that they shared was predictable and hilarious at the same time.

I heard Lovelle's laughter at Shantell's typical morning banter.

"Hush Shantell," I said as I wanted to hear everything that Lovelle was saying. Shantell walked directly to her favorite place in my house: the refrigerator. Knowing she would be occupied for a few, I continued into my conversation with Lovelle.

"Long time, no hear stranger"

"I know, Baby girl. How have you been?"

At that point I wanted to focus in on the Baby part, but I just continued on like I didn't catch it."What puts me on your mind this morning?" I asked.

"Lunch." he responded.

"Lunch? You do know it's breakfast time?, Better yet, what did you think.'Oh ham sandwich, Cindy'?" I said with laughter.

"No, actually, I wanted know what you were doing for lunch." he said. I paused for a second. What did he mean, I thought he was still in Canada. "Cindy, did you hear me?"

"Oh, I'm sorry. Shantell was making noise. Could you repeat that?"

"Can I take you for lunch? I can be there in a couple of hours."

I must have gone straight into kiddie mode with my smile because Shantell picked up on it.

"Oh, look at you! What is your husband telling you? she said loud enough for Lovelle to hear her.

"Would you stop calling him my husband, I ain't got no ring on my finger." I said with a blush.

"Not yet,"I heard from the other side of the phone.

"Excuse me?

"Just be dressed at 11:30. I will be there then."

"What he say?" Shantell asked as she threw herself across my couch.

"Aaahhhhhh,'' I said in a tiny squealing voice. as I found myself jumping in place like a little girl."I got to get dressed he is coming to get me. We going for lunch."

Shantell grabbed my hand and we both begun jumping in place like little girls.

"Girl, I told you y'all weren't over!" Shantell says as I headed toward my bedroom.

"Lunch, Lunch, what do I wear to lunch? Brown…no. Black …no. Ooh jackpot." I pulled out a pair of jeans, a cute pastel blouse and a blazer. "Yes do it, but don't over do it. I said to myself. I couldn't believe that the thought of seeing him gave me the same jitters as when I was 13. But it felt good. I loved it!

As I was getting ready to jump into the shower, Shantell knocked on the door and said, "Call you later C, we've got some moves to make I want to run by you. Don't let him kidnap you," she said laughingly.

"Ok," I answered. Well it's not like I've never been kidnapped before. But I definitely wouldn't mind if Lovelle did it!" I found myself in consistent grin as I lathered myself with sweet scents.

He called me "baby." And what was that "not yet" part about? While all of these thoughts raced through my head I wondered did it mean that he wasn't with anyone anymore? I had to have myself calm down, because I knew how I could get. Besides I would know in due time I figured. 11:30 wasn't far around the corner.

By the time I was putting on my finishing touches on and applying my lip gloss, Lovelle was right on time. At the knock on the door, I grabbed my telephone, acting as if I were speaking to someone. I didn't want to look too anxious.

"Hey, Missy, looks like your ready on time for a change," he said.

"In case you forgot, Lovelle, I was born ready," I said smiling.

Lovelle looked so good. I don't know what that Canadian air had in it, but it really worked with him. Not wanting to waste too much time I grabbed my things and went for the door. Outside was a white Lexus, but not wanting to assume how he had gotten over to my house, I asked if I was driving.

"No, I got this," he said as he approached the Lexus. As he opened the door for me he said,"Your chariot awaits."

I laughed as I remembered in my youthful fantasies, he came and rescued me on a white unicorn. Yes a unicorn. I had a very vivid imagination.

I watched him as he entered on the driver's side, taking the opportunity to really soak him in. I had noticed a little extra weight but it looked good on him. He still had his basketball physique that I always found so sexy. But something seemed much more mature about him for some reason. To be quite honest, as confident as I portray, his demeanor was a little intimidating. I had to question was he he too sexy to be with me? Was he now too far out of my league?

Anyways, I shook off my daze to fully participate in the conversation that he had begun. With every question we asked each other out loud, the real questions I had went unasked.

Questions like "Where is your girl?" and "How long are you staying in New York?"

Yet instead of asking what I really wanted to know, I just held them to myself, hoping to stumble across this important information later in the date.

Well the afternoon went wonderful. We ate lunch at this Mexican restaurant and laughed and talked like the olden days. Still, there was little said about him being involved and to be quite honest, it wasn't as important as it first seemed. What seemed more important was the fact that no matter how long we kept away, we could always get things right back to where we last left off.

Lovelle was special to me. He knew Cindy Maze. Not Treasure or any of the other alias or personas I had created.

We rode to my house where he had dropped me off. The only thing that felt unusual about the date was the fact that instead of kissing me on the lips, he he gave me an lingering kiss on my hand.

My mind could try to analyze what that could have meant, but I knew it would drive me nuts. Time would have to figure that one out. Whether it was his way of saying we were just friends, or what? But like I said, I had to leave that in time's hand.

I already had so much on my plate, and shortly after unlocking my door I realized I had three new messages. The first was Parker, the other was Shantell telling me change of plans and the last was Mr. Jesse telling that everything was set to meet Little Richie on the coming Saturday. He also told me if I had a change of heart, to let him know. I knew there was no way of that, so I paid that no mind. I don't know why this man questioned me so much, but I just took it as he really cared for my brother. Besides I couldn't think of any other reason he would go out of his way to double check my intentions if he didn't.

I spent the rest of my day handling business, which all seemed trivial compared to the other things on my mind. In fact, money was the least of my concerns for the first time in as long as I could remember. Even still, it seemed as much as I earned I still felt no growth. Easy come, easy go!

The following morning I realized I hadn't heard back from Shantell so I called her. She answered in a groggy voice which told me she had a long night.

"Whats up with you Shantell?" I asked.

She laughed and responded sarcastically, "The same thing you and Lovelle could have been up to!"

I should have expected this from Shantell. By the sound of her good mood, I knew she was not with the baby's father. She was never happy when she was with him, only when she was with Tyson.

Confirming my intuition she told me that she and Tyson spent the whole night at the casino.

"The casino? Why wasn't I invited?" I asked with a giggle.

"Private party, Girl. Private party," she said.

She continued to tell me that she had a proposition for us. Usually when she said this , it meant something real over the top or Al pacino style. Shantell was like this, and her sense of dangerousness she felt while dealing with Tyson, I already knew this would be interesting. I told her to get dressed and meet me at 3pm. Shantell already knew how I felt discussing things over the phone, and especially around Tyson.

A TEST OF LOYALTY

Shantelle and I eventually met up, but later than scheduled. Shantelle has always had a unhealthy relationship with time. so I let it go. But as usual she jumped into the car mid-conversation.

"Wait, wait, Shantelle," I interrupted. "Why you so fast?" I asked as if I were astounded.

"Why you so slow?" she answered in a giggle. "Are you ready to get this money, C?"

"Why, what's going on?"

"Tyson said…"

"HOLD UP! Tyson?"

"Yeah, C, don't start. Tyson knows these guys who have a shady trucking company."

"Ok, Shantelle, this is already starting to sound crazy!" I responded.

"No its not!" she answered defensively.

"We don't have to do anything but drive this truck to this place and drop it off."

"What's in this truck, Shantelle?"

" It's gonna be furniture and things. Of course it's gonna be others stuff in there but…"

"Oh really, now we a moving company? What's in this for us?" I anxiously asked.

"Ten thousand dollars."

"Whoa, that's a lot of money. What's the catch?"

"Come on, C, it's not like we never did stuff like this back in the day."

"Yeah, Shantelle. Remember why we stopped?"

"Come on, you can't compare two young black girls driving an expensive car to two woman looking like they are moving. What's more suspect?"

"You're driving!" I smirked.

"Oh really, that was then! Come on, C, it's not like imma be speeding in a moving truck," she laughed. "In fact you can drive."

"Really, so where is this drop off and when?"

"It's in Florida, and it's this weekend."

"Shantell, that's about a day of driving?

"Damn, C, why you acting so private eye? It's a simple job with a big pay. They are paying us to drive that far!"

"Let's not be delusional, Shantell. They are paying us to risk our lives. Besides, this weekend is no good for me."

"Is ten thousand dollars not enough to be without Lovelle?"

"Where are you coming from with that, Shantell?" I asked showing my attitude.

"Naw, nothing, C. You just acting different right now. Why you can't come?"

"If you had been paying any attention lately, Shantell, you would know I am supposed to meet up with my little brother this weekend. Actually on Saturday."

"Yeah, C, ten thousand dollars. You can postpone that?"

At this point, I had gotten really upset. That's just when my heavy breathing began. "Really Shantell, postpone seeing my brother? Now I know you're crazy!"

As she continued to push the issue I begun to get even more angrier. To me it begun to seem like she was so selfish that I questioned how real of a friend she was. She knew that my brother was my everything, so why was she acting this way?

Eventually things escalated and I put her out of my car. I never had to do that before, and I felt bad. It's strange because all while she was speaking, I no longer heard Shantell. All I heard was Tyson speaking through her. It is no secret of how I felt about him. But now, I was even more turned off. But foremost in my mind was that she needed to stop talking because I had enough. I didn't need to hear from her until she came to her senses.

All throughout the day I thought about Shantell and our conversation. Trying to decide which part bothered me most. Was it the fact that she was so caught up in Tyson's greed that she was beginning to make foolish decisions? Or was it her not volunteering to be at my side when I met my brother? Either way I was disappointed. I still felt the need to make sure she didn't move forward with that job, but I figured she probably wouldn't do something so big without me being her wingman.

To be quite honest, I wasn't into taking the kind of risks like I usually would. Although it was faint, I was beginning to see the glimpse of a better life for myself. I had already opened up to the possibility that there was another lifestyle, one that was less dangerous and stressful out there for me.

It took time, but I had cut off a lot of my connections in the game. Especially those that seemed a little more shady than others. Real estate seemed like the most likely of my options. Parker agreed that was one of the most profitable hustles at the time, so I was very interested. With very limited education, even I could figure my way around with a little help. Besides, I would begin as an investor anyways. Crazy, but no longer was I alright with being a ghost to society. Also, how far could all the partying and booze get me anyway. I was so tired of losing!

THE LONG OVERDUE

Friday approached and I still hadn't heard from Shantell. I was really becoming concerned with what she might do and with whom. But being who I was, stubborn, I refused to make the first call. Besides I felt it was her fault that we argued in the first place. We weren't usually at odds with each other, but sometimes even sisters go through things. It just had to be dealt with in time, I felt.

Besides this on my mind, Lovelle had offered to take me out fordinner. He told me there was something really important he wanted to talk to me about. I asked was it something that could wait, but he insisted that it wasn't. I agreed to meet him but I hoped it wasn't going to be something crazy because after fighting with Shantell and the rest of the things on my plate, I definitely didn't want an issue with him also. That just would have been too much heading in the wrong way for me.

My nerves were on edge for my meeting tomorrow. Thinking about the fact that Richie Boo was a teenager, I wondered how I should approach the whole situation. I wondered if would he still be the sweet little man he was when I saw him last, or if he had grown to have the same attitude toward life as I had.

I really wanted to bring him something, but couldn't figure out what. He was way too old for a Tonka truck, and when I was his age I was more into clothes and stuff. Was he a chip off the old block or was he one of these tech kids that seemed to be popping up everywhere? I wished I had known how much he had grown, that would have made everything so simple. All of my curiosity made me even more anxious. Really, I just hoped he would like me. I just wanted to make a good impression.

Friday evening came at a wink of the eye. I was confirmed for what I thought would be a typical dinner date with Lovelle, but being my nerves were kind of bad I didn't put to much effort in preparing myself. In fact, I was in jeans and flat shoes. something he had never seen me in.

I don't know, but it seemed that I always dressed in a way, but ultimately he never seemed impressed. At least he rarely commented. Instead, he would compliment me when I felt the most undone. Lovelle was just that way sometimes. You never knew if he had noticed or intentionally made you feel he hadn't. Ironically, he counted my every smile and always knew when something was on my mind, so it was a little safe to say he paid attention to certain details.

Lovelle oddly, asked me to meet him instead of picking me up at my house. Something else that he had never done before. This made the evening more suspicious to me. I mean was I downgraded so much in his life that picking me up and dropping me off was too much?

While driving to meet him, I was thinking of many things. Part of me wanted to turn back, fearing this would be extra stress added before an important day, and the other part of me wanted to meet Lovelle in person to take my emotions back.

He had been a little different since he had returned. It almost seemed he wanted to have his cake and eat it too. Maybe it was the time to let him know the buffet was closed.

Unfortunately, I reached the destination before I had the chance to make up my mind. So I guess the decision was made for me. My thoughts were distracted by the fact that I realized the location I was at. This was one of my favorite places in Brooklyn. It was City Line, where I loved to walk the boardwalk and watch the boats dock. Now I was thinking the night might not be so bad after all. I guess Lovelle remembered how much I enjoyed seafood. So sweet, I thought.

I wished that I hadn't already eaten. Yes I know, most people wouldn't eat knowing they're going to dinner. But it's just something I would do. I never wanted to appear greedy on a date, also just in case the date was not going smoothe, I could get up and leave before the entree. Crazy I know, but it was just my logic.

Luckily for me there was parking right across from the restaurant. More confirmation that this night might not be so bad. As I stepped out of the car I noticed Lovelle coming out of the door of the restaurant. As he got closer, I was able to really check him out.

He was wearing a crisp white button up, a beige jacket and dark pants. It's not that he usually didn't look good, it's just that he looked extra sexy to me. He made me wish I would have worn something different, but hey, whatever I wore I always look good I figured.

He walked over to me with smile and a hug. "Hey Missy, thanks for coming out."

"Of Course," I said as I felt him kiss me on my cheek and I murmured, "Real sexy."

"What? Me, or the restaurant?" he asked with a conceited smirk.

I laughed, wanting to say definitely "You!"

"Well, Cindy, it seems our reservations got a little mixed up. They are packed in there. The next table will take at least another hour. So, we can grab somewhere else or wait. It's up to you."

I looked at the other restaurants and said, "We can wait."

Inside I was thinking, good thing I ate. He pointed to a well lit area of the boardwalk and said, "Let's grab a seat over there."

"Cool with me," I said.

I kind of enjoyed looking at the water. It was always very relaxing to me. I usually would find the water when I need to clear my mind of some things. Especially drama. As we walked across the street, he put his arm across my back the way that always made me comfortable. It made me remember when we were together.

"Whats going on with you, Cindy?", he asked.

"What do you mean, Lovelle?"

"Is there anything you feel I should know ?"

Inside my mind I said,"There's a lot you don't know. Especially about me!" but still I played ignorant and asked, "What do you mean?"

He pointed me to sit on the bench, angled himself toward me and looked me directly in the eyes. "Cindy, we've known each other for quite some time. Sure, there was a lapse in time but we've made up for a lot of that wouldn't you say?"

"Of course, Lovelle, but what is this all about?" I asked sweetly yet impatiently.

"Hold up Lady, I'm getting there... I just wanted to know if you were interested in trying to to take our relationship somewhere different?" There was a pause that followed. He squeezed my hand and said, "Cindy Maze, I love you!"

At this moment of shock, my heart went so fast that my spirit felt like it left me. Where was this conversation going? I wondered. And what could I do NOT to ruin this for the second time?

"So, Cindy, I asked again is there anything that I need to know about you?"

I knew the quick answer would be to say "No" but my face began to show both delight and concern, and as good as my Poker Face was typically, I couldn't keep it together. I felt caught. It seemed there would be no right answer to follow.

If I said "yes" and started to tell him about the lifestyle I had hid from him so long, I was afraid he would look at me as a total liar. If I said "no," wouldn't he eventually find out, and think me to be even more of a liar because he didn't learn it from me?

In my turmoil my body broke away from him, as I felt the warmth of my breeze blown tears. Cindy, don't let a tear fall, I said to myself. But it seemed out of my control because they rained.

"What's up, Baby?" he asked.

"Lovelle, I can't have this conversation right now."

"Cindy, what do you mean? I am telling you I love you and your shutting me down again."

He was right. The first time I totally spoiled it, and almost lost him doing so.

"What is it?" he asked. "What am I overstepping Cindy? Is there someone else?"

At this moment of his questioning I knew he was really concerned and the next move was on me. I reached back for his hand and I began to speak the words I hoped I wouldn't regret. "Lovelle, I'm not the same girl you knew in high school. Since then, I've been through more and done more than you could imagine."

I began to see his face change from concerned to confused. "What do you mean, Cindy?" he asked. "Why are you so distraught?"

" I want to tell you about a lot of things, Lovelle. I just don't know how," I said.

Lovelle squeezed my hand and wiped away my tears with his outer hand. "Cindy, how about this?, how about I be plain with you. Do you know Rudy?"

"Yeah, why?"

"Well, Rudy and I used to ball together as kids. I went on to play overseas and he kind of let it go, but we always remained cool. How do you think I got in contact with Shantell?"

It's funny how I never put two and two together, but now I was really curious to where this conversation was going. He continued to say he had been asking around about me for years, but no one but Rudy ever had information.

"He trusted me enough to tell me the full ordeal of what you came through and what you and his cousin were dealing with. Please don't be mad at him, really he was looking out. He said if I couldn't handle it, don't even come in your life to bring more grief. He thought you had enough. I gave him my word, and that what brings me to this moment."

"So if you knew, Lovelle, why all this time you never say anything?"

"I guessed a secret worth hiding was a secret worth keeping, Cindy. I hoped you would trust me enough to be there for you one day. Knowing your lifestyle gave me pressure though. I knew I had to get financially straight to be enough to support you."

"So what kind of things did he tell you I was into?" I asked anxiously.

"Lets just say the type of things I won't say in public," he laughed.

"So what are you saying Lovelle? You're alright with it?"

"No, Cindy, I'm not alright with it. I'm just saying I understand. It always had me worrying about you. It killed me I couldn't just tell you to stop. But I'm just saying that if you were willing to be my wife, that all might be easier to change."

Just then my heart skipped again. He could tell by how I froze that as easily as he slid that in, I was still alarmed.

"Hold up," I said. "What did you just say?"

"I said you won't have to worry about money!"

"No, no, what else did you say?"

"Oh, you caught that?" he said and smiled.

"Was it worth catching?" I asked.

Lovelle pulled away, which really threw me off. There was a moment of silence and he stared deeply into my eyes. I don't know who should break it, him or me. Did I really want to hear his response, I wondered. Maybe he will tell me he misspoke and kill the whole dream I had in that moment. Instead he reached for his pocket, my eyes locked in on his every movement. I was immediately attracted to the vivid color that he pulled out of his pocket. I would have known that color anywhere. Even the glare of the lamp post could not distract from the brightness of the ole so famous Tiffany blue box.

As I stood from my daze, he asked me, "Was this worth catching?" and before my eyes was the most beautiful ring.

I couldn't believe it. Was this for real? The tears began to restore to my lids. This time they felt as cool as rain drops. My smile formed with the emotion of joy partying inside.

For the first time I didn't have anything to say to mess up the moment. No sassiness, no arrogance. Nothing, just speechless. Lovelle's face looked as if it were glowing as he knelt to one knee.

"Now, Cindy, I ask you once more. Is there anything you have to tell me?"

"Yes. Yes, I will be your wife," I said.

And just like that the ring was slipped unto my finger. Wasn't this the most beautiful moment I had ever seen? It was almost too good to be true. I almost thought that fate would remember that this was Cindy, that this was happening to, and snatch back the moment.

"Oh tough girl...you're mine now!" he said in laughter.

Lovelle kissed me in a way that made me feel that I could be made brand new in that moment. We continued that night unto the morning. Each minute greater than the last, and no matter what, I believed in this moment. Even a broken clock is right twice a day!

It was only hours away from seeing my little brother, and no matter how perfect the night was, it didn't take away from the fact that I was anxious. It seemed in just twenty-four hours my whole life was forming meaning. And as upset as I may have been with Shantell, she was one of the first people I wanted to speak to in the morning. I knew that if I told her that Lovelle popped the question she would probably be happier than I was. Yet after several calls to her, I got no answer.

I began wondering if she was ignoring me or something. I was nervous for some reason, and nervousness is not something I'm used to. I wondered how could I have this terrible feeling in my belly when everything that I had looked forward to was just hours away. Either way, this would have been one of them times that Shantell would have talked me into another planet and I would have forgotten to feel this way.

Anyways, I went home to get myself together for the day. Being typical Cindy, I was confused as to what to wear and wasn't sure what impression I wanted to give off. Would it be a hip-hop look? Did I want Little Richie to meet a hip looking big sister, or did I need to give off a more conservative vibe? One which showed his big sister could be responsible and handle things.

It's funny, but even when I looked in the mirror, I looked like a newer person. Besides the anxiousness in my brows, I had this other look about myself. I practiced the faces I would make when I saw him. Trying to imagine the Cindy he would meet again for the first time. Some of which made me giggle a bit. Cindy, it's not that serious! I had to remind myself. I had to just accept that there was no real preparing for this day. I just had to let it happen. Meanwhile, I was getting sweet messages from Lovelle, wishing he could have joined me for this occasion. I also received the message from Parker saying he was on his way. Parker and I had both agreed, that should this day ever come, he would be by my side. Sometimes it's good to have a big brother-type around. He had this way of making me feel safe and comfortable.

I made myself as busy as I could until Parker came, and when he finally arrived he must have read my expression because he said immediately, "C, Relax." I laughed at him being able to read me so well. But as the time neared for the appointment I didn't know how to control myself.

I wanted to tell Parker about last night with Lovelle, but I wanted to save it until I could give him the full run down. I wondered how he would take it though. Would he say I was jumping in head deep by accepting or would he think it was a good natural progression? You just never knew with Park, and though I shouldn't care about his opinion, it did matter. But I guess I figured he would notice the ring and we would go from there.

As we rode on our way, we listened to the same ole old school station we always did. Luckily, the station was playing all of our favorites and we sang along as usual. Some of the songs reminded me of the life I lived before everything went tragic. Especially those which reminded me of Lovelle. This was just the type of ease I needed going into this situation of reuniting with my baby brother. The humor of Parker's non-singing self-hitting forbidden notes was all I needed to lighten up the air.

Before I noticed we were in front of the place. And there was no turning back at this point.

Inside, I new this visit would bring upon a different me. An accountable part of myself, a woman. Just in the midst of thought here came Mr. Jesse to let us into the building.

"Hello Cindy," he said with a smile.

"Hey," I replied. But there he was with that strange look again. The same look he gave me last time. I thought,"Something is wrong with this man!"

"Well Cindy, I'm going to ask the two of you to sit in this conference area across from my office. I'm actually waiting for some guests. And Richard, of course. Make yourselves comfortable."

I agreed and we walked into a room that had a long table and chairs, but had a comfortable looking couch sitting against the wall that I opted to sit on. I didn't want it to seem like a school meeting or anything formal, so I figured this would be more cozy.

As we were sitting, I heard voices in the hallway. One of them definitely was Mr. Jesse, and as the sound came closer I felt my palms sweat and my throat get dry. Parker put his hand on my shoulder in effort to calm me. But anxiety was quickly setting. Suddenly I saw a hand open the door. It was Mr. Jesse saying,"Cindy, we have some people who want to see you."

When he spoke, I couldn't help but to notice he said people. I mean was Little Richie with his foster parents or something? I wasn't really prepared to talk to anyone else at that point.

Then, in midst of my thoughts there stood a tall, handsome, slender young man. There were other bodies standing around as I stood to greet him but I could hardly make out any of the faces, since I was totally focused in on him. I was just amazed!

"Richie Boo?"

"Sis," he answered back.

"Oh my goodness you're so handsome."

His slightly muscular arms reached into a bear hug. My head in his shoulder, I felt the moisture of my tears on his collar. As I embraced him a lot of memories raced through my head. Memories of me holding a little boy that thought the world of me. Memories of feeling protective of him, and above all, the feeling of belonging!

I had not felt the flesh of my own blood in years. Suddenly I was no longer an outcast with no connection. I had family; he was it.

He finally backed way and I was able to gather a better look at him.

"Why you crying, Sis?" he asked.

"Why you crying, Little Man?" I said with a slight giggle.

He giggled along, as he said he was so happy to see me again. I smiled of course, because that was all I ever wanted to hear him say. Those words made my heart feel light.

I examined him, and as hard as it was to admit he really looked like his father. Although nothing made me want to say this aloud. Suddenly the environment opened up and I began to notice my surroundings. I really wasn't ready for the shock that I had encountered.

The face of a woman I only just became aware of pierced me, and I began to stare at her. She said nothing, but her face was smeared with makeup from crying along. As I came to myself I realized it was Denise. My mother.

I quickly looked over to Mr. Jesse with a face both of confusion and anger. As I asked "What is this?" he said no more than, "Let me explain," before I began to mouth words to this woman known as my mother that I never thought I could say. The tension in the room escalated as Parker unknowingly jumped to my defense asking, "What's going on? Who is this lady?"

Little Richie began to look nervous as he saw a part of me that he was not familiar with.

"Calm down Cindy. Let us explain," Denise said.

"Explain What? …Who asked you to be here? I know I didn't! I wanted my brother, that's it, and all!!" I hollered.

Mr. Jesse reached for my shoulder as he asked if I would have a seat. By this time Parker had realized what was going on and asked me to do the same. I supposed it was too much for Little Richie because he left the room. Once I noticed this I asked Parker would he go and get him for me.

Regardless of my true emotion, I knew I would have to be civil enough to listen to how all this came about. But within the details came the shock of my life. Little Richie came to sit by me, as he showed the sadness in his face.

Denise began to speak of all the changes that had occurred in her life. And suddenly the whole story I was told about my little brother had been changed. As it turned out, there were no foster parents responsible for my brother. The whole thing about him being placed here and there was made up. Mr. Jesse explained that he was told that that story may bring upon a easier way to make this reunion happen.

Although I was happy to be reunited, the lies really upset me. True, maybe if I had known my brother was involved with Denise, I would have probably been uneasy with the whole situation, but I'm sure something would have been worked out eventually.

But the biggest shock was yet to come.

Denise began to tell me that Mr. Jesse had been working to make this happen for years. She said the reason she was clean for all of these years was because of him and they have been together for years now, raising Richie Boo.

I looked at them all and suddenly the picture came together. But where did I fit in? So with the few words I had in me I asked the question.

"So Denise and Jesse, since everything is so perfect in your world, why after all this time, am I here? Obviously, Little Richie is not leaving here with me, so what's up?"

That's when the ultimate was spoken. She said,"Jesse really wanted to meet the daughter that he never got to know."

"Stepdaughter!"

"No. Daughter, Cindy," she said.

At this point I looked at Parker. He looked back at me confused with the question in his eyes of "What the hell did she just say?" I beat his question to the punch and asked, "What the Hell did she say?"

Inside I knew exactly what she said, but I needed her to be direct with me. And she was, she said, "Cindy, Jesse is your biological father."

At this point I knew I had officially heard the craziest thing in my life. I don't think I was ready to hear anymore. My face must have showed how finished I was with the conversation, as Denise and Jesse Both looked at a total loss for speech. I just gave them the hardest stare and I gathered my things to leave. Midway through the hallway, I felt a tug of my arm. Luckily, I didn't just swing without looking because it was only Richie Boo.

"Richie, whats up?"

"Sis, please don't leave again!" he said in a humbled voice of concern.

"I have to, little man. This is too much, but I will see you around! I'm glad to see you're doing well. That's all I ever really cared about."

"But Sis…"

"Lil Bro, we'll have our time soon. I promise. I love you!"

I gave him a kiss on his forehead and I turned around hoping to be quick enough before another tear fell.

The ride home was filled with all the rants I could possibly think of. I exploded all my frustration about what I felt, toward Parker.

My Nana used to say, "Still waters run deep." And though I had no idea of what she meant back then, I think I finally understood at this moment. Every timeless hurt that was suppressed suddenly found its way to emerge.

I hid most of this hurt successfully for years. I hid it behind designers and perfumes. Now, here it was. Parker tried his way to chime in with a little bit if encouragement but even he was unsuccessful at calming me down.

For as much as I had shared with him about my life, I don't even think he knew the extent of my pain. I was good at acting like I had a handle on things. But meeting a father I had never known, in this way, was too much. Sense totally blocked the mention of him out of my life. I didn't know: should I be happy or angry? Besides, he, too, had abandoned me. Where was he when I needed him? If either one of them had been true parents, I wouldn't have the scars of my life that I have now!

LIFE DOESN'T PAUSE…IT CAN ONLY BEGIN AND END

The craziness I felt exhausted my emotions. After a while my brain went quiet and it all began to settle in my head. I now questioned my anger. I mean, had not a small part of me wanted this throughout the years? What happened to the optimism I used to have? Cindy, Let it go I said. Just let it go!

Pulling in front of my place Parker's phone began to ring. I was still irritated, not only did I not want to speak, but I didn't want Parker to speak to anyone either. I wanted Parker's full participation in my misery. But he answered his phone anyway. He didn't say much to the person on the other line. But he said ,"I got you!" to the person and hung up.

I looked at him to get an explanation for why he took the phone call and since he felt he had to who was it?

He just stared at me and said, "C, we've got to go!"

"Go where, Parker?" I asked.

"You'll know, once we get there!"

His voice had an unusual tone I hadn't heard in a while that concerned me. We began to ride off again. Realizing he was paying no attention to the stop signs and lights, I knew something was wrong.

"Park, What is it?"

He acted as if he didn't hear me or just didn't want to answer. His whole expression was bland. It almost seemed like I was being driven by a ghost. Needless to say, this put the stress from what happened earlier the furthest from my mind.

We zoomed right into the emergency entrance of the hospital. Suddenly his silence was broken as he said in a choked up voice, "C, Shantell is here. Let's go now!"

He caught me totally off guard. I would usually react off pulse, but it took a minute to register what he said. By the time it computed, I was watching him run inside the double doors.

Following him in shock, I turned the corners of the hospital, until before my eyes I saw the face of my best friend surrounded my doctors and nurses. Parker looked at at me at the very moment he knew I realized what I was looking at, because he charged at me with an embrace. I felt my heart drop and out came the biggest scream. I could not control my outburst. It took over the fullness of my body.

I have heard people talk about the moment when they realized too much was enough, and I felt that I had finally reached that point. Looking at Shantell in the state that she was in, and with all the skeletons that fell out of the closet earlier in the day, I felt powerless. More than I had ever felt before. I experienced a frozen moment when my body and my soul had separated from devastation.

Nothing that anyone could ever tell me would have me to believe that the worst things to have happened to a human, had happened to me. In a surreal state, I heard Parker call for nurses to come to my aid. I guess he saw that I was fading. Before I knew what was happening, I was on the floor of the hospital with lights blurring around me and roars of voices calling my name. Suddenly the sound disappeared and I was behind a cloud of white. I had passed out!

I laid in what seemed like a eternal rest until a face broke through to me. It was Shantell.

"C, Girl what's that on your hand? Congratulations, Girl!" I heard her in her usual high pitched tone, but for some reason her mouth did not move a bit.

"Shantell, Girl! what happened?"

"Girl don't worry about that, I'm good!"

"I was calling and calling you, why didn't you answer me?" I asked.

"C, you know I'm a busy body, but I got you. Cindy, do you got me?" she said as her tone became more tranquil.

"Yeah, Girl. You know that! What's up?"

Whats up? I asked three times, but she said nothing. Her face just began to get this golden type of hue like the time time she had just finished swimming. I don't know why, but I felt myself weep.

"Shantell........Talk to me. Talk to me!"

I then heard in a soft vibrating tone. "I Love you Sister!"

And just like that she faded to be replace with a beeping sound.

I opened my eyes to see myself on a hospital bed, with IVs attached. Lovelle sat on a chair next to me, and Parker not far off to the side. I sat up to look around. My first words being, "Shantell... Where is she?"

Lovelle squeezed my hand with a slow shake of his head. Parker came over an sat near my foot, looking like he had aged 10 years. I had to listen to them tell me that my best friend was no longer alive. How could I ever prepare for that. My emotions felt like a black hole, and with every tear I sunk in deeper. I felt stuck.

Months and years of one day began from that moment. Although I was told I participated in laying Shantell to rest, I can't say I really remembered. I guess my body showed up but my soul had not returned to the morning that I was confronted by Shantell mother and Rudy about my godson. I was faced with the option of taking custody of him. I was shocked that they were asking me. They explained that I was the most suited, and they knew that Shantell would have preferred it that way.

It was just then, that I guess I came back. I knew that was the thing that I had to do. Protect my godson. I knew Shantell without a question would have done it for me. I had to be the one to love him through the absence of his parents.

I knew the most what it felt like to be alone, and I did not want him to ever feel that way. With a mother gone, and a father in jail for life for killing her, I knew one day he would question his place in this world, and I need to be there to help him.

My Little Shawn..... I vowed I would be there for him until the last of me.

Indeed, it took some years, and a life adjustment. But Shawn had what I always wanted. A bunch of love around him. He had me and my husband Lovelle, Uncle Parker, Rudy, the Dawsons, Lil Richie and ironically Grandpa Jessie and Nana Denise.

Yes, as hard as it may be to believe, over time this all came together. I can't tell you the day forgiveness came into my heart, but I guess it snuck in when I thought I had lost the heart I used to have.

Either way, I am in love with the life of Cindy King.

Where life had gone years after the pain was amazing. My life had transformed in a way I once couldn't imagine. It seems there was a dropbox for pain at that church I visited. Afterwards, I had begun to yearn to hear from that resounding voice, and I did. I began to notice pieces of my pain fall away.

The Street life I don't regret, but I don't miss it either. I learned that every bit of my trials was worth it to be in this place. Part of my healing was seeing Denise for who she was and more importantly understanding that she was just human. We all make mistakes and it's what we do with them that matter most!

Will we let them define us, or will we grow from them? Now I spend my days behind this desk watching these stories and futures run through these hallways. Right across from Jesse. I had the thought to remove my door off the hinges because I never wanted any of these young people to feel it was not the time to come in. Many Little Cindys have sat in the chair before me. I'm their Mrs. Dawson, I'm there Nana, I'm their support. Plaques of unfinished business hang from the walls. Graduate…CINDY KING. Although none of it came easy, it was surely these tests that lead to my testimony.

Hopefully, one day When Lil' Shawn or this baby in my stomach ask me the question of how I made it through, I can let them know…it was all by the Lord's GRACE.

My path will never be forgotten. And although a stranger may meet Cindy King…the worshipper, the wife and mother, friend and sister, student and teacher.

I will undoubtedly remember the prayers of my Nana, and proudly say, that I am still,

"A MAZE IN WAYS."

THE END

DEDICATION

This book is made in dedication to my Grandmother, the late Mrs.Gladys Harris. Because of her encouragement and belief I was able to start the first pages to this book. For this among many other reasons, "Thank you Mumma".

To my Mother Lillian Harris and late Father George Ford, I hope I make you proud.

My Brother Taiwan and Sisters Toni, August and Corina, this is for our dream.

And to all my family and friends, I Love you!